AN ANGEL'S TOUCH

A midlife paranormal thriller

MEMORY GUILD BOOK 10

WARD PARKER

Mad Mangrove Media, LLC

ISBN: 978-1-957158-18-1

CHAPTER 1

BAD DOG

I am the human vessel of Danu, the ancient Celtic earth-mother goddess. And guess what I was just doing? Healing the earth? Making flowers bloom?

Nope. I was scrubbing aluminum cookie sheets, trying to remove the charred remnants of a batch of scones that I burned yesterday. And no, the Goddess did not give me the power to make the rock-hard carbonized crust disappear. My middle-aged arm muscles had to achieve that feat, and even using steel wool, this arm wasn't up to the task.

Welcome to my world: that of a woman with paranormal abilities, a goddess inside of me, and a day job as an innkeeper at the Esperanza Inn, with a to-do list that never gets shorter. Still, I'd rather just be me, Darla Chesswick, than the human incarnation of a goddess.

I made the dough for today's scones—I use pastry flour, which gives them a lighter texture. I also chill the dough before baking. Once this batch was out of the fridge and into the oven, I went out the front door of the inn to collect the five copies of the daily newspaper I have delivered each morning to leave on the foyer table for our guests.

Oh, but the indignities continued.

This morning, I found a bigger-than-usual landmine waiting for me outside.

Cory and I don't own a dog, but I had to clean up dog waste nearly every day. That's because Mister Pookie, a 200-pound mastiff, loved to leave a present outside our door. Why? Because his owner was irresponsible and let his dog run around without a leash, even though our historic neighborhood was as far from open fields as you can get. The dog could've also had an issue with me or a very human-like sense of humor.

I won't gross you out with details, but Mister Pookie was especially prolific this morning. In fact, I needed a shovel, as if I were cleaning up after a parade of elephants. And, even stranger, Mister Pookie's output was glowing red like embers.

My supernatural instincts began tingling even before I sighted the actual culprit trotting away down the next block. It wasn't Mister Pookie. The brief glimpse I had of its hindquarters before it turned the corner told me it was the largest dog I'd ever seen, with a body built like a Rottweiler but several times bigger.

The dog's tail was very odd, though. At a distance, it looked almost like a snake.

Something wasn't right.

A woman shrieking from around the corner confirmed that.

I raced down the street and turned right, like the dog had done.

The elderly neighbor looked familiar, but I didn't know her name. She stood shaking with fear, holding a severed dog leash.

"The monster took my Shelby," she sobbed.

When I reached her, I put a hand on her shoulder.

"I'm so sorry," I said. "That huge dog attacked yours?"

"It wasn't a dog. It was a monster. A hound from Hell."

That described Mr. Pookie, in my opinion, but he would never eat someone else's dog.

High-pitched yapping heralded the return of Shelby with half a leash attached to his collar. The woman scooped up her dog and showered him with kisses.

Unlike most people, I had regular encounters with creatures from Hell. So, I had to ask, "Could you please describe the monster?"

"A gigantic, dog-like beast with three heads and yellow eyes! I can't get the image out of my mind of one of its heads grabbing my Shelby."

"The trauma probably made it seem like the dog had three heads. I don't know if a birth defect of three heads has ever been recorded in mammals before."

I said that simply to tamp down her confidence of her recall, to make her doubt her own memory. We couldn't have people spreading rumors about supernatural creatures.

However, I was very confident in the accuracy of her memory. I believed the beast *had* been a three-headed dog.

Namely, Cerberus, the hound belonging to Hades, the God of the Underworld. Cerberus obviously was the latest creature who had slipped into our world through a tear in the Veil separating us from the underworld.

I glanced at my watch. No time for hunting mythological monsters. I must cook breakfast for our guests.

A sleepy Sophie made her appearance as I was transferring the scrambled eggs from the skillet to a chafing dish.

"Good morning," I said, resisting the urge to comment on how tired she looked. She had probably been up late with her boyfriend, Haarg. There was talk of the two getting married. I was not thrilled by the prospect of having the Fae God of War as a son-in-law.

"Morning, Earth Mother," she said.

"I don't need the sarcasm. I just had to clean up the excrement of Cerberus from the sidewalk in front of the inn."

"Cerberus? Isn't that Hades' hound?"

"Yep. I see your schooling has paid off. He passed through the tear in the Veil and is now running around San Marcos. Animal Control can't bail us out of this."

"Maybe Haarg can help us. If I remember the legends correctly, wasn't capturing Cerberus one of the Twelve Labors of Heracles?"

"I think so."

"Haarg would love to one-up Heracles. After breakfast, I'll connect with Haarg and ask for his help."

"Good." I handed her the chafing dish to carry into the dining room. "It beats you having to fight Cerberus with your magic sword."

Sophie and I had defeated monsters from the other side of the Veil before by simply destroying them, as Sophie did to a cyclops. More frequently, we've transported them back to Hell or the In Between with the help of gateways, which I now knew were angels.

Destroying a mythological creature like Cerberus, of whom there is presumably only one, didn't seem right. It might not even be possible. He would need to be sent back to the gates of Hell, and a god, such as Haarg, should be able to accomplish that. Besides, the Fae tore the Veil in the first place, so let a god of theirs deal with it.

My phone rang. It was Detective Samson.

"A report came in about a three-headed dog chasing seagulls along the bay," he said. "Do you know anything about it?"

"You automatically assume a freakish situation involves me?"

"Yes. I know you too well."

"Okay. I saw him at a distance. I believe he's Cerberus."

"Who? Is that a new breed like the cockapoo?"

"No. He's from Greek and Roman mythology. He's the dog that guards Hell. He must have come through the rift in the Veil."

"Well, if he's supposed to guard Hell, he's abandoned his post. That means there could be a massive jailbreak from there. Darla, I truly don't want an invasion from Hell coming to San Marcos."

"There is a connection between the opening in the Veil and San Marcos that I don't understand. But if creatures from Hell come here, they'll hopefully just be passing through on their way to Washington, DC."

"How can you be so snarky at a time like this?" he asked.

"It's the only way I can keep my sanity. Don't worry, Sophie and I will take care of this."

"Immediately, please. We can't afford for any tourists to be eaten."

"Gotcha."

After I ended the call, Sophie went upstairs to summon Haarg and get her sword, just in case. I summoned Cory from the workshop to supervise the breakfast service.

The bay was only a block away, and I drove along Bayfront Avenue as slowly as a tourist while Sophie and I looked for signs of the hound from Hell.

"When is Haarg going to get here?" I asked.

"He said right away, but you know gods have a different sense of time than we do." She looked at me and giggled. "Than I do."

Having the Goddess in me did not alter my sense of time. I

had an inn to run, with such duties as Teatime, which could not begin late.

"If Cerberus is supposed to guard the gates of Hell, why would he want to come here?"

"I don't know. Maybe he's like a dog who runs off for the simple joy of it. No, I take that back. This monster doesn't seem like the joyful type."

"So he's not here for the tourist attractions?"

"No. I'm afraid he's here for the tourists."

A flock of seagulls erupted from the seawall along the bay-front promenade. A giant creature leaped atop the wall. It had three heads and a snake for a tail. Each head held an unfortunate bird in its mouth.

"He does seem joyful at the moment," I said, as I stopped the car across from Cerberus. "How do we contain him until Haarg gets here? And keep him from being spotted by tourists?"

It was still early since I must rise at the crack of dawn every day to do my chores. The tourists weren't out strolling along the promenade or walking to the entrance of the historic fort yet.

But wait—a jogger was approaching along the promenade from the south, heading toward Cerberus.

The three-headed dog saw the woman. He wagged his snake tail and coughed up feathers.

"Sophie, we need your magic. Fast."

She lowered her window and pointed her sword at the monster, murmuring Latin words I couldn't make out.

A thin bolt of purple lightning shot from the sword and touched Cerberus. The creature froze.

"An immobility spell," Sophie said. "Pretty cool, huh? First time I successfully cast it. I'm more used to blowing things up."

"I know. But turning monsters into exploding goo isn't the

solution to every problem. Do you have a way to make Cerberus invisible before he's seen by the jogger?"

The woman was about to come around a slight bend in the path and would soon have the monster in her direct line of sight.

"I have a cloak of invisibility. But I only know how to put it around myself. Let me try something."

She jumped out of the car and ran to the frozen monster.

"Be careful!" I called out after her, as if my daughter were at a playground and not armed with magic and a sword, charging toward a mythological monster.

A car pulled up behind me and honked, jarring me back into the real world. I drove forward and parallel-parked. When I looked at Sophie again, she was standing beside the seawall, with no sign of Cerberus, who was presumably right next to her within her cloak of invisibility.

Her spell had worked.

I joined Sophie on the promenade just as the jogger passed by. The woman didn't seem phased at all to run past a woman with a sword. Living in a town where re-enactors dressed in seventeenth-century garb had its advantages.

The air around Cerberus shimmered slightly, allowing me brief glimpses of his hideous, muscular body.

"Your spell seems to be weakening," I said.

"You always criticize my work. I'm doing the best I can."

"When is Haarg getting here?"

Sophie sighed with exasperation. "When he gets here. He's a god. No one rushes a god."

She silently mouthed his name, becoming just as impatient as I was.

A low whistle came from the north. A male bodybuilder wearing only a loincloth and sandals was checking out the jogger as she passed him. Haarg in human form.

Sophie hissed with jealousy.

He paraded toward us, shoulders thrown back, tossing his long black hair behind him. A large dog collar and leash made of chains were in his hand. He beamed when Sophie met his eyes.

"Where's the little puppy?" he asked, giving me a peck on the cheek like a dutiful future son-in-law.

"Right here, beside me," Sophie replied. "You can't see him? I didn't think my spell would work on a god."

"A god in human form," he said defensively.

"I also cast an immobility spell on him. Which I can break when you lead him away. Or you can just transport him like this back through the Veil."

"First, I must wrestle him and make him submit to me. Then, he will wear my collar under the control of my leash."

"Wrestle him?" I asked.

"In human mythology, Heracles captured Cerberus with his bare hands. As a god, I can do nothing less."

"You can just whisk him away from here," I said. "The sooner, the better."

"No, no. I must fight him and prevail through courage and brute strength."

"He's right about the brute part," I muttered.

Haarg crouched and flexed his biceps. "Release the hound."

"Right here in public?" I asked. "Can't you fight him in Hell like Heracles did?"

"I refuse to handle a creature rendered helpless through magic. Release him, Sophie."

Sophie waved her sword and uttered something in Latin.

Cerberus abruptly reappeared, fully mobile and lunged at *me*.

I screamed and jumped backward, just missing the jaws of his left head. Why me?

Unfortunately, my scream attracted the attention of an

elderly couple across the street. They looked over to see a guy wearing only a loincloth jump upon a three-headed giant dog.

This wasn't going as I had intended.

Sophie and I had to step off the promenade as Haarg and Cerberus thrashed about on the cobblestones. The god attempted to subdue the creature using traditional wrestling holds. Every time he secured a head, he had two others with snapping jaws to contend with.

Haarg screamed in pain when the dog's snake tail bit him in the butt.

Cerberus bucked the god off his back, and now the god was on the ground with the dog atop him, three mouths going for his throat.

Haarg seized a dog throat in each hand, but the center head chomped on his face. Meanwhile, the tail bit him in the hip. Haarg thrashed desperately.

"I think I should help him," Sophie whispered to me.

I shook my head. "It would dishonor him to be saved by his human girlfriend."

"I don't care. I don't want him to be eaten in front of me."

The elderly couple across the street stood there, staring at the spectacle. The wife held her cellphone to her ear, while her husband appeared to be shooting video with his phone. I knew the video wouldn't capture the monster, so I wasn't worried about that. I was afraid the wife was calling 911.

"We have to get Cerberus out of here before the police and more witnesses show up," I said.

"We have to save Haarg from being mauled."

"Shouldn't a god be able to win?"

"Cerberus is Hades' hound. I guess that gave him god-like powers."

"Heracles beat him."

"Mom! That's just an old myth."

So was the very existence of this three-headed dog. Yet here he was in San Marcos. In public.

Haarg wriggled out from beneath his foe and leaped upon his back. It looked like the tide had turned.

Until it turned again. Somehow, Haarg ended up back on the ground with his head in one mouth and the other two mouths on his neck and shoulder. The creature's tail sank its fangs into Haarg's thigh.

The last time we had watched Haarg in battle, he hadn't been able to beat the Father of Lies. It looked like he was going to be zero for two.

"Yes, I think you need to intervene," I said.

Sophie pointed her sword and cast the same spells she had used before, making Cerberus immobile before he became invisible.

Haarg groaned and pulled himself out from beneath the monster.

"What did you do?" he asked with a whine. "I was just about to defeat him."

"I'm sorry, honey," Sophie said, "but tourists are showing up. We need to get Cerberus out of San Marcos. Can you please take him away now?"

"You shouldn't have used your magic. Now I can't claim that I was victorious."

"Honey, if we're getting married, you need to accept that we're a team of equals. There is nothing wrong with us defeating Cerberus together."

"But it should have been my triumph."

"It's *our* triumph."

"You have dishonored me."

"You were getting your butt kicked."

Uh-oh. Their path to connubial bliss was looking mighty rocky right now.

"Please, Oh Mighty Haarg, take Cerberus back to Hell," I pleaded with extra humility.

He huffed and put the leash and collar on the invisible monster.

"I'm going to walk this dog right in front of Hades to rub it in his face."

He disappeared.

"The Veil needs to be fixed," I said. "I can't go on dealing with monsters all the time."

"I think men are just as difficult to deal with," Sophie said.

CHAPTER 2
YOU FIX IT

"That was one monster who wasn't too difficult to take care of," I said as we drove home. "I'm grateful to Haarg for taking him back to Hell."

"Yeah." Sophie brooded. "Haarg and his inflated male ego."

"You're the one who chose the Fae God of War."

"He chose me. Lucky me."

Was she souring on him? I hated to admit it, but I wished she would. Nothing good ever came of mortals hooking up with deities.

"Speaking of deities," said a resonant voice behind me.

I glanced in the rearview mirror. The archangel Raphael, in human form, sat in the back seat with his legs crossed. He was wearing a white tunic, with no sign of his wings showing, and was as gorgeous as ever.

"Oh, hello." I hoped my breathless voice didn't give away how much his beauty overwhelmed me. "After all these years of being transported by gateways—not knowing they were angels—

I'm now transporting an angel. Sorry my car's such a mess. Definitely not suited for a celestial being. Oh, and do you mind putting on your seatbelt?"

"The lesser angels serve as what you call gateways," Raphael said. "I'm here to deliver a message to you from the Big Guy."

No need to ask who the Big Guy was.

"Is this about the Veil?"

"Exactly," the angel said. "It must be healed as soon as possible. It has been damaged for far too long."

"Everyone has been pestering me to fix the Veil. The guilds of San Marcos, the Fae, and you. No one has ever explained why it has to be me. I'm not the least bit mechanically inclined. I'm not at all handy around the inn. Cooking and baking are skills I have. Sewing? Not at all. I'm the last person you want repairing a veil between two worlds."

"Is that what humans mean by joking?" He smiled, and the angelic light glinting from his teeth nearly blinded me. "You are being called upon because you carry the powers of the Goddess Danu. You have the power of healing. And you protect the health of the earth."

After Raphael had begun visiting me, I researched him and learned he was traditionally associated with healing. No wonder he was obsessed with Danu and restoring the Veil. But why would God have an interest in an ancient Celtic goddess? I asked Raphael this.

"All gods and goddesses are parts of him," the angel replied. "The names and personalities humans have given them throughout history mean nothing to him."

"And how do you know it's a 'him'? What if it's really the Big Gal?"

Raphael smiled again, causing me to avert my eyes.

"Human speech is so limiting. Guy or Gal makes no difference. God is beyond gender. As am I."

That threw me for a loop. I was attracted to this gorgeous angel, and he's gender fluid?

"I am a celestial being," Raphael explained. "I am not of the flesh. What you see is the form I adopt when interacting with you, based upon your idealized conception of an angel."

Idealized was right. He made me tingle in spots I didn't even know I had. He said his physical appearance was only an illusion. But isn't that what romantic attraction was all about?

"You're attempting to change the subject," Raphael continued. "We were discussing your mission to repair the Veil."

"And I was questioning why I would be chosen to do it. I'm a simple, ignorant human who happens to be the vessel for a goddess who has been absent from the earth for thousands of years."

"Danu has never been absent. She is part of the earth, as the earth is part of her. She has been present more now than ever, trying to heal this planet of the damages from humans and the Fae."

"Why don't you make the Fae fix the Veil? They're the ones who damaged it."

"Yes, that is true. They tore it open with the help of the Father of Lies. Perhaps we shall assign a faerie to work with you."

I wasn't so sure of that. The only faerie I could think of who might be helpful was Baldric, a local resident and member of the guilds—not a participant in the Fae's failed invasion of North Florida and the southeastern US.

"I want to be clear," I said. "I don't know how to fix the Veil, and I'm doubtful I have the power to do it. Even if the goddess pumped me full of power."

Raphael wasn't smiling anymore. His expression was stern.

"You will learn how to fix it. And you must not fail. I will be honest with you—this mission will require great sacrifice on your part."

Nice job persuading me, Raphael.

"What if I refuse?"

"You must not—cannot—refuse. This is your destiny."

"My curse," I muttered.

And just like that, the angel disappeared from my back seat.

"What did he mean by sacrifice?" Sophie asked.

"I don't want to know."

THE MEAL BEGAN SILENTLY, WITH ONLY THE CLINKING OF cutlery and plates. Cory, Sophie, and I sat at the small table in the dining nook of the cottage where Cory and I lived. The two bedroom, one-bath home had been built in the 1920s to accommodate families staying at the inn. Now, it was our permanent residence and where we had family dinners in a more private, intimate setting than the large formal dining room in the inn's main building.

"Can you resign as the human incarnation of Danu?" Cory asked.

"I don't know," I replied after I swallowed my bite of chicken. "I've never understood why or how I was chosen for this role."

Back when I found I could communicate with trees and they called me 'mother,' Wilference and another faerie priest told me I resembled Danu's depiction in the Fae's ancient religious artwork. And I'll admit, when seedlings began sprouting inside the inn, I began to accept that I had something to do with it. Discovering that I had healing powers was the real bonus, but when I learned I had the limited power to destroy harmful entities, I never dreamed I'd be called upon to use that power.

"You've spoken to Danu, right?" Sophie asked.

"Sort of. When I'm in a dreamlike state. But she never tells me much. The ghost of Birog, the Druid, is a bit more helpful with specifics. But she mostly just nags me and tells me I need to figure things out."

"And you can't recall any encounters with Danu before this began?" Cory asked.

"Nope. Didn't even know who she was."

"Did you study ancient Celtic mythology in college?"

I shook my head. "It's like the goddess just spotted a human who vaguely resembled her and said, 'You're hired.'"

No, that is not true.

The Spanish-accented voice that sounded in my head belonged to the black cat, Cervantes, who lay on a nearby windowsill, staring at me. Previously, the witch's familiar only communicated with my witch family members: Cory, and Sophie. Not me. But now that I had the goddess in me, I could hear him telepathically, just like the others.

"What do you mean, Cervantes?" I asked aloud.

I sense that there was something early in your life that presaged your connection with Danu. It wasn't random. It was your destiny.

There was that word again. Destiny. "Like what?"

I don't know, Darla. It's my intuition telling me. You must discover the answers on your own.

"I thought this cat was good for more than catching mice and lizards."

Cervantes appeared to be smiling at me in a cat fashion.

The way Sophie and Cory stared at Cervantes told me they had heard what he'd said, too.

"Do you know how Darla can fix the Veil?" Cory asked him.

The cat was silent.

"Just because he's a familiar doesn't mean he knows everything," Sophie said.

Cervantes chirruped in agreement.

"You know, I don't care how I came to Danu," I said. "I accept Cory's suggestion. I want to resign."

He and Sophie gave forced smiles.

"Raphael said that I would have to make a great sacrifice. I don't want to. I've already had to sacrifice a lot, thanks to the supernatural. Same with you two. Why can't we just be like normal, boring people? Why can't we run our inn in peace? I mean, just my psychometry alone is a tremendous burden on me without counting my duties with the Memory Guild. And think of all the crazy stuff that has happened in San Marcos with me right in the middle of it?"

"That's what I've been telling you forever," Cory said. "Let's just pretend we have agoraphobia and never leave the inn again."

"The inn has a gargoyle, a vampire, and several ghosts staying here," I said. "We can't avoid them."

"That's okay. I feel like they're part of the family. What I don't want is you being attacked by faeries and three-headed dogs. Why can't you just quit it all, like I stopped practicing magic?"

You've stopped practicing it, but you're still a witch, Cervantes told him. *Magic will be part of your life forever.*

Cory sighed and speared a green bean with his fork.

And the supernatural is woven into the fabric of your being, Cervantes said to me. *Fighting malignant supernatural beings and using supernatural powers for good are your destiny.*

You had to hand it to our cat: he had a good vocabulary.

"Enough of all this talk about destiny." I swallowed the rest of my red wine. "I'm deciding what my destiny is. To live my life as a normal person. I can't turn off my psychometry, but I can ignore everything other than my family and my inn."

Cervantes opened his mouth but made no sound. I think it was a laugh.

"I refuse to repair the Veil," I added. "Let someone else deal with it."

As I was preparing for bed, my phone chimed, indicating someone had rung the bell at the inn's main entrance. After each evening's wine social, and after I finish my daily chores, I switch on the security system that requires a key card to enter the main entrance and the other exterior doors. If someone rings the doorbell, my phone alerts me.

I put my clothes back on, and as I crossed the courtyard to get to the main building, my phone buzzed with a text.

Samson identified himself as the one at the door. I replied I was on my way.

Of course, I assumed it would be bad news at this hour. Based on Detective Samson's expression, I knew I was right.

"I need your and Sophie's help," he said after I turned off the electronic locks and let him in.

"Is this about a monster?"

"You guessed it."

"What happened?"

The attack happened earlier that day, so I knew Cerberus

wasn't responsible. Samson said a professor from the local college was hosting a party at his home, and a guest was abducted. The party attendees described a gigantic male lunatic who smashed through the door of the home, knocked people aside, and grabbed a philosophy professor. The attacker ran off with the man over his shoulder.

"How do you know it was a monster?" I asked. "It could have been a man having a psychotic episode because of drugs."

"We found the victim's remains. He had been devoured."

"Oh." I'd heard of attackers who were high on bath salts trying to eat their victims' faces, but not the entire victim. "Why is this a job for Sophie and me?"

"I think it's a monster that slipped through the Veil. The host of the party is an expert in the legends of Old English, Old Norse, and Old Germanic. He said the attacker was a monster like Grendel."

"Who?" The name was familiar, but I couldn't place it.

"The monster from the Old English epic poem, *Beowulf*."

Now, I remembered. In the Dark Ages, the monster, Grendel, repeatedly attacked a mead hall in Scandinavia, killing and eating warriors. Until the hero, Beowulf, came along and killed him.

"Sophie and I are like Beowulf?"

"Well, Sophie is, with her battle magic and her sword. I still can't get over how she destroyed the cyclops at the fortress. I was hoping she could take care of Grendel the same way. Preferably, before anyone realizes we have an actual monster in our city."

"Would it matter if I told you I was retiring from the supernatural business?" I smiled weakly.

"No. You know as well as I that we can't allow people to be

killed, and we can't even allow them to know a monster is doing it. Remember, we must maintain secrecy about the supernatural world and maintain the equilibrium. Besides, this city depends on tourism. Monsters eating people leads to bad ratings on the online review sites."

"True."

"I need not just Sophie's magic for destroying the creature, but also your help in finding it before it kills again."

"How am I supposed to do that?"

"With your psychometry, of course. Didn't you once track down a vampire that way?"

"Yeah, but—"

The heavy glass door of the main entrance swung open—the door I had unlocked to let Samson in. And forgot to lock again.

A hulking figure stood in the opening, silhouetted by an exterior light.

The dark form was male and humanoid. He was covered with thick fur on his chest, shoulders, and lower regions. The hairless areas were shiny, reptilian scales. The face was more ape-like than human, with a slightly protruding snout that dripped saliva. Yellow eyes burned beneath a heavy brow. Two short but sharp horns protruded from his temples.

His nostril slits opened as he sniffed us. He focused his attention on me and crouched, ready to spring.

Grendel was here.

I telepathically screamed for Sophie to come with her sword. While I could pick up thoughts at times telepathically, sending my own thoughts was never a guaranteed success. But if Sophie didn't hear me, hopefully, Cervantes would, and he'd wake her.

Samson stepped between me and Grendel, pulling his handgun from its shoulder holster instinctively, as any trained law-enforcement officer would do. But then, he forced himself to begin the shapeshifting process. As a werewolf, he would have better luck against the monster.

I put myself into the semi-trance mode that allowed me to connect with the Goddess. Her power was needed to pacify the creature. Or to destroy him if the Goddess deemed him to be a perversion of nature. He certainly gave that impression to me.

It was taking too long for the Goddess's powers to fill me.

Grendel leaped at Samson.

And there was no time for Samson to complete his shifting.

I held my hands out, palms facing the monster, trying to stop him like the Goddess had helped me stop faerie arrows and hostile vampires.

But nothing happened. Grendel didn't stop.

Samson fired his weapon in the split second before the creature bowled him over. It looked like the bullet hit the monster's thigh.

The innkeeper in me was about to ask Samson not to shoot anymore and awaken the guests. Instead, I screamed.

Grendel wrestled Samson, trying to hold him while his giant animal jaws went for his throat. Samson, with visible fur, but nowhere near wolf form, wriggled out of his grasp. He attempted to get another shot off.

The creature knocked the gun from his hand, sending it sliding across the ancient oaken floor.

I tried again to clear my mind and connect with the Goddess. Instead, my instincts made me grab a heavy ceramic planter and break it over Grendel's head. The soil and pottery shards showered over Grendel and Samson while they struggled on the floor.

The creature was on top of him, gaining control over his prey.

Divine Danu, please give me the power to stop this creature.

The familiar burning sensation began deep in my abdomen. Energy radiated outward, reaching my arms.

The painful nature of the burning meant the power was not for healing or calming. It was for destroying an abomination of nature. An entity that was like a cancer, threatening the natural species of the earth. Grendel was not a normal predator, a carnivore who sustained himself with meat. He was a murderer who killed out of hatred.

Samson screamed. Blood gushed across the floor as the creature's teeth sank into the detective's shoulder at the base of his neck.

My fingers burned, and white lightning bolts arced from them, hitting the monster in the head. He fell backward, looking at me with confusion. Then his expression turned to anger as he came at me.

I sent lightning at him again, but he was too close to me, and I hit him with only a short burst before I stepped backward and tripped over the umbrella stand. I landed hard on my butt, the monster looming over me.

He reached down for me before being knocked backward by a thick bolt of purple lightning.

Sophie had arrived in the foyer, sending her magic from the point of her sword.

She screamed something in Latin, and Grendel flew backward, crashing into the reception desk.

And I had thought it was a waste for her to take Latin courses in college.

Grendel knew he was outmatched. Crouching low, he ran toward the door as Sophie aimed her sword at him, gathering the energies to fire another blast.

He pushed through the door and disappeared into the night.

Samson groaned. He lay on the floor in a puddle of blood

that expanded like a rising tide. I feared an artery had been nicked.

"Call nine-one-one," I said to Sophie.

"I just did."

Dropping to my knees, I changed my psychic focus from harming to healing. I pushed my hands against the gaping wound, pushing the ragged edges of skin together as Samson's blood leaked between my fingers. His recently sprouted fur had disappeared.

"Please don't die, Michael. Please heal him, Danu."

Warmth spread through me again. This time, it was warm, but not burning. It flowed into my heart and down my arms. My hands tingled as it spread into Samson's flesh.

And the flow of blood dwindled.

The bleeding stopped. It was a miracle.

No, it was the healing power of Danu.

Sophie brought a first-aid kit from the kitchen, and we did our best to clean and sanitize the wound before covering it with lots of gauze and tape.

Finally, paramedics arrived and took over. Samson was unconscious now, his face frighteningly pale from the blood loss. But the rise and fall of his chest told me his breathing was strong and steady.

A police officer walked in. Great, it was my frenemy, Fernandez. She was visibly shaken by the sight of Samson being placed on a stretcher. I hoped that meant I wouldn't face her usual sarcastic comments.

"The carnage at the Esperanza Inn continues," she said. She just couldn't resist.

"We haven't lost a guest in quite a while," I said.

"Good for you. What happened to the detective?"

"He stopped by to warn me of a dangerous lunatic in the

area, and the lunatic broke in and attacked." It was only a partial lie, one of omission.

"Can you give me a description of the lunatic?"

Now, I had to lie more broadly. I made up a loose description of a marauder who was like a cross between a pro wrestler and a popular comedian who I will not name.

"The whole thing was so traumatic and happened so quickly that my description might be a bit off," I said.

Fernandez nodded knowingly as she scribbled on a notepad. "He sounds like a cartoon character to me."

"Or a character from an Old English saga," I said.

She looked at me quizzically, then told me a detective and crime-scene techs would arrive shortly. The San Marcos Police Department would spare no effort to find the man who assaulted one of their own.

Not to mention a college professor and who knew how many future victims.

The paramedics left with Samson, and I pulled Sophie aside in the front parlor.

"They couldn't promise me Samson would make it," I said. "This has gone too far. We can't allow any more creatures to escape through the Veil."

"I thought you were washing your hands of this."

"I wish I could. But someone must stop the monsters. And by someone, I mean you, too."

"I wholeheartedly agree," said a male, English-accented voice.

The stone gargoyle beneath the fireplace mantel had animated.

"As long as you're on board, Archibald," I said with maximum sarcasm.

"I'll back you up all along the way," he replied. "With advice, from a safe distance, of course."

"I would expect nothing more."

As much as I wanted to shrug off the cosmic responsibilities that I felt had been unfairly placed on my shoulders, it appeared I had no choice.

The earth mother in me would have to save the earth.

CHAPTER 3

PRACTICE RUN

The following evening, Birog appeared like she often did, as a reflection in my bathroom mirror. It looked like she was standing behind me. I caught a whiff of a noxious perfume, but she was not present in a material sense.

Only in an annoying sense.

"Well, are ye about to step forward and accept yer responsibilities?" the Druid's apparition asked in her archaic Irish accent.

"If someone explains to me what exactly I'm supposed to do," I replied.

"If anyone knew that, the Veil would have been repaired by now. We need ye not only for yer goddess powers, but for yer noggin'. Ye're the one who's got to figure this out."

"I don't know where to begin."

"Well, I be here to help ye."

"How reassuring."

My sarcasm didn't anger the Druid; it only made her chuckle. That was probably a good thing because I didn't yet know if this ghost could harm me. She didn't look stable, with the flowers and leaves braided into her hair, the triskelion tattoo on her neck, and the bizarrely applied ancient version of makeup that made her look like an aesthetically challenged Goth chick. Her teeth were stained black, too, for some reason.

"First, ye got to strengthen yer connection with the Goddess. Ye need more of her power, and ye need to know all the ways ye can use it."

"So far, her powers have helped me heal the Faerie Queene. And Samson's nicked artery. I've had some luck repelling attackers and zapping creatures that are corrupted and unnatural. The problem is my powers don't always work. And I don't understand how they operate. I feel like I've jumped onto the back of a galloping horse with no way to control it."

"Aye. 'Tis understandable."

"When I visit the Goddess in visions, she never gives me specifics. She wants me to fix the Veil—just like the angels do—but she hasn't told me how to do it."

"Ye can't depend on a goddess to be your instructor. That will be my role."

"But you've never instructed me, either. When you've visited me before, you've told me to get my act together, then you disappeared. No helpful instructions at all."

"Divine powers aren't like that." Birog seemed perturbed. "They're miracles. Wonders. Incomprehensible to human minds."

"That's not good enough for me to figure out how to fix the Veil."

"Did anyone tell ye how to do the magical acts ye described doing?"

"No. I just did them."

"Well, there ye go."

"No, no, no. We're not talking about deflecting arrows or zapping vampires. The Veil was created by God, I presume. Age has weakened it over time, which makes me believe it's organic, or at least is subject to being worn down like inanimate materials. Powerful magic created by the Fae was then able to damage it. This is a major, complex undertaking. I can't simply show up at the Veil and hold my hands out to repair it magically. Plus, how the heck do I even show up there?"

"Stop yer whining. Let's find something that's a stand-in for the wall and see if ye can repair it."

"The wall separating my courtyard from the street has a big crack in it. That's hardly comparable to the Veil, but I can start there."

"Let's go, girl. I'll meet ye there."

I SAID GOODNIGHT TO CORY AND WENT OUT INTO THE deserted courtyard. The side of the three-story inn facing it had only two windows with lights on: Sophie's and a guest's. Once again, I was one of the last people awake. And would be the first up in the morning. No wonder I was suffering a major sleep deficit.

The crack in the wall was barely noticeable from the street side, but here in the courtyard, it looked bad. The walls were made with blocks of coquina quarried from the beach hundreds of years ago. It was a type of limestone comprised of tiny, shelled creatures that compressed together over several millennia. The city's fortress was made from the same material; the stone was sturdy, but soft enough to absorb cannonballs from the pirates and other invaders without cracking or shattering.

However, being in the elements and the salt air for a few centuries will lead to cracking from embedded moisture and the like.

"Ye really think this wall is anything like the Veil?"

Birog had appeared beside me.

"Well, it's all I've got at the moment. The Veil acts like a wall," I said. "The time Raphael showed it to me, it seemed to be woven from fibers of some sort. This is just stone. But its basic minerals came from the shells of living creatures."

Birog grunted with skepticism. I didn't care. I was here, so I might as well see what I could do.

I cleared my mind and took deep, slow breaths. Getting into a meditative state was easy in the darkness, with the only sounds being my breathing, the trickling of the courtyard fountain, and, far away, the clopping of a horse-drawn carriage carrying tourists.

When the familiar warmth spread through my center, I placed my hands on the wall over the crack. Nothing happened.

Then my psychometry kicked in. I picked up recent thoughts from Cory as he studied the crack, wondering how to repair it. He considered bolting metal plates across the crack to prevent the fissure from separating more and causing this part of the wall to tumble down. Concrete would be poured to fill the crack, though the color wouldn't match at all.

Bad ideas, Cory.

Then, I picked up a random memory from decades ago. A young newlywed leaned her back against the wall late at night. Her hands were at the small of her back, palms pressed against the coquina—

—while Tom kisses me passionately and presses his body against me.

Everyone else from the wedding party has finally gone to bed, and it's time for us to—

Whoa! Too much information. I hadn't intended to use my psychometry; it just happened as it always did. Shutting it off wasn't easy, but I needed to focus on the Goddess's power.

I deepened my concentration, attempting a better connection with Danu.

Birog thankfully remained silent, except for three words:

"Use yer senses."

Sounded like reasonable advice. After all, I didn't know what else to do. Focusing on my sense of touch and feel, I hoped to get signals from the stone like I previously had when sensing the electrical activity in forest roots as the trees communicated.

Of course, rocks don't communicate. Well, maybe they do with Archibald. As a stone-speaker, he could learn the history of this coquina, but wouldn't be able to tell me how to meld it back together.

I continued pressing my hands against the coarse texture of the coquina, packed with tiny ridges, traces of miniature seashells embedded in the whorls and peppered layers of stone. It was like a hardened concrete made with nature's recipe and cured for thousands of years.

And then it happened. I picked up on all the energy residing in the stone—from the mollusk and gastropod shells that formed it, to the power of the millions of waves that had beaten against them, grinding them down and mixing them with beach sand, clumps adhering together, covered with fresh sand, working their ways deeper below the surface of the beach.

When the ocean rose and covered much of Florida, the rocks were far underground, where freshwater springs flowed around them, depositing more minerals as larger and larger formations of rock formed.

Thousands of years later, when the ocean receded, this coquina was beneath the beach. Storm after storm pounded the shore and washed away sand, until the coquina formations were exposed once more to the sun, rain, and salt.

Eventually, humans discovered it. The Spanish colonists, beginning in the 1500s, quarried it and carted it to the mainland to use in building the new garrison town of San Marcos.

A couple of hundred years later, it was used to build this courtyard wall.

While the history of this stone was revealed to me, my other senses learned even more about it—knowledge that couldn't be put into words because it was beyond human comprehension. It was not complicated; it was the simple essence of the stone and its inherent energies.

And, somehow, I was becoming one with this inanimate object.

I understood it down to the molecular level, down to the elemental level.

Why the wall had cracked was clear to me now: too much water absorption. And how to heal it was plain as day.

The rush of power that surged through me and out of my hands shocked me. It wasn't fast and sharp like when I attacked with lightning bolts. It was slow and steady, like the tides, gravity, and the other primal forces of the earth.

The ancient song of the Goddess—the one that had repeatedly filled my head when the Goddess fully possessed me—came from my mouth as I hummed it at a low volume. No one could hear my humming except for Birog, but the music powered me. It was a song I could not name, but which was eternal and universal.

It was a song of healing, of mending, of making things right again.

A low, grinding, scraping sound came from the wall. The cobblestones vibrated beneath my feet as the stone shifted. And, sure enough, I felt the fissure in the wall shrink from a quarter inch gap to nothing. The blocks of coquina were now solid, continuous stone. Seeing it clearly, despite the darkness, I could discern no sign of a crack at all, not even a hairline.

"Ye did it," Birog whispered. "There's hope for ye yet."

Her voice broke my trance, and my senses returned to those of a normal woman in her courtyard at night.

"This is nothing, though, compared to fixing the Veil," Birog said.

"Of course. I know that. The angel told me that fixing it will require a great sacrifice on my part. Do you have any guesses as to what he meant?"

"Only guesses. Like, ye might have to give up your life as a human."

"You mean die?" I asked to deaf ears.

Birog had disappeared.

I GRABBED A FLASHLIGHT FROM THE COTTAGE AND INSPECTED the wall. Not to pat myself on the back, but the repair looked perfect. From the street side and the interior side—where the fissure had been glaringly wide—the wall looked like it had never had a crack at all.

Imagine if I had gone with Cory's plan of filling the crack with concrete. The brand-new filler would have stood out terribly amid the dark, weathered coquina. Magic has its benefits!

I went to bed pleased with myself for using the Goddess to

accomplish the task. Fixing a crack was such a trivial, material thing. It didn't involve life or death, health or illness. You'd think the Goddess's powers wouldn't apply to menial jobs like this. But I had successfully harnessed them and made them work.

This was a major step forward in learning how to repair the Veil, whatever it was made from.

I felt a benign presence in my bedroom and opened my eyes. Cory was sleeping beside me, so it wasn't him.

"You are making progress with your education," a voice whispered in my ear. It was Raphael. "Your journey is still long. Soon, you will receive a visitor who will help you with your assignment. A faerie, because the Fae engineered the rending of the Veil and must help repair it for justice to be served."

"Who?"

He didn't answer, and I felt his presence fade.

I hoped the faerie would be Baldric or someone else who was highly skilled in magic. Magic had created the damage, and it might take more power than the Goddess's to fix it properly.

After my excitement finally wore off, I fell asleep. And had worrisome dreams about what kind of sacrifice I would be required to make.

THE NEXT MORNING, I WAS BACK TO SLAVING AWAY AT TASKS far beneath a goddess's pay grade. You know, get the newspapers, check for dog poop, bake scones, prepare the rest of breakfast, check online bookings that came in overnight, cajole Sophie into trying a little harder to help me, listen to Cory complain about the maintenance of a nearly 300-year-old inn. The usual.

A few hours later, I barely noticed the old man at the front desk who looked like he had just stepped out of a medieval monastery.

Good grief, it was the faerie priest Wilference.

"Hello there," I said, feigning joy at seeing him. "I hope you're not here for those belongings you left behind in your room. We had to dispose of them. They smelled rather horribly."

"No, Daughter of Danu," he said, bowing reverently. "That is not why I'm here. I've been assigned by the Faerie Queene to assist you in repairing the Veil."

My heart sank. No, of all the faeries in the world, I had to get this guy? It wasn't fair.

"Are you absolutely sure you're the one who was assigned?"

"Oh, yes. The Queene commanded me in person at her winter palace in Palm Beach. I'm supposed to give Fae insight to help you on your mission."

"Wonderful," I said through a smile so strained I think I pulled a facial muscle. "We'll make the perfect team."

"When do we start?"

"I don't know yet. Actually, I don't have a plan at all. First, you'll need to tell me everything you know about how the spells that tore the Veil were cast. Do you have this information? Or can the Queene send someone else?"

"I have sufficient knowledge about how it was done. I'll share it during our strategy sessions. I expect we'll need several sessions."

"Well, I've always been the kind to just wing it," I said.

"No, no. One cannot wing it when dealing with celestial architecture. We'll need to do a great bit of strategizing. Which room am I staying in?"

Please save me, Raphael. Last time Wilference stayed here, he completely trashed his room and did worse to the bathroom.

The foul stews he cooked in the fireplace damaged the paint in the hallway, as well.

"We're completely sold out," I lied. "Sold out for weeks on end," I lied, more egregiously. "We might have to put you up in temporary quarters. Like in the utility room."

"As a priest, I need no luxury."

He's lucky I'm not forcing him to camp outside, I thought.

CHAPTER 4

LOSE THE DARLA IN YOU

When Fernandez called me, I expected sarcasm and cold questions about the attack by the intruder, whom she didn't know was a legendary monster named Grendel. Instead, she had uncharacteristic fear and sadness in her voice.

"Just thought you'd want to know," she said. "Detective Samson has taken a turn for the worse."

"Oh, no! What's wrong?"

"I'm not sure. They said he's not recovering properly. Something about an infection. You might want to visit him."

I asked Sophie to take over the breakfast service, her eyes showing she knew how upset I was. The hospital wasn't far away, and I hurried inside to the front desk. Not being a family member of Samson, I had to persuade them to let me see him.

He was asleep in his bed, several IV lines hooked up to him. A plastic tube fed oxygen through his nose. A nurse and a tech were in his room.

After I introduced myself, the nurse told me they were about to move him to the Intensive Care unit.

"But why?" I asked. "I thought he would recover fine from his wounds."

"They are bite wounds from an animal the doctor believes was carrying an unidentified disease similar to rabies," the nurse said. "Though the intake paperwork says he was attacked by a human. Human teeth couldn't have caused that wound."

"Is the wound not healing?" I asked.

"It's healing, slowly. But the infection is spreading throughout his body. It could lead to organ failure."

I fought back the urge to cry. The attack wasn't my fault, though in a way it was. Grendel passed through the Veil, which I hadn't repaired. And he came to the inn. Originally, the faerie Jaekeree's magic had directed the monsters to come after me. The Fae wanted me dead and believed only mythological monsters could kill a goddess. Obviously, they weren't successful, and after Jaekeree was defeated, the monsters that slipped through the Veil came after any humans.

Yet, many were still drawn to the inn. It must be because the Goddess's energy was there. I believed that was why Grendel went there. To kill her. He just happened to arrive when Samson was there. It was unlikely the monster was following the detective.

Samson had put himself in harm's way because he came to see me.

As I stood beside my sleeping friend, I noticed the nurse and tech had stepped out of the room. It was my brief window to put the Goddess's healing powers to work again.

Against the sound of Samson's labored breathing, I cleared my mind and went into a meditative state.

"Goddess Danu, please empower me," I whispered.

I pictured the old-growth forest where I had visited her

before, the towering trees, and the forest floor covered in ferns. The roar of the waterfall. I didn't see her; I *was* her.

The familiar heat began deep in my abdomen and spread throughout my torso. It was a powerful heat, but not painful like when I gathered the Goddess's energies to attack an enemy. Her healing energies were almost pleasurable instead.

I placed my hands atop Samson's head as the heat flowed through my arms and hands into him. The words of an ancient song burst from my lips. The melody was achingly familiar, but I couldn't identify it. And the words were in a language I couldn't comprehend, but I knew they were meant to heal and soothe.

Eventually, all the heat inside me passed to Samson, and the song died on my lips. I studied his face, looking for signs of improvement. The lines on the EKG monitor didn't seem different. The monitor said his heart rate and oxygen level hadn't changed. He remained unconscious.

So now what?

"Was that you singing?" the nurse asked.

I looked over at her standing at her computer cart, the flush of embarrassment flooding my face. It was a decidedly different kind of heat from that which the Goddess caused.

"Um, I guess."

"Are you very religious?" she asked.

"You could say that. In an unconventional sense."

"I believe the faithful are helped by prayer."

"Yeah, I guess you could say I was praying in a fashion."

"I'm afraid we're going to move him to the ICU now. Since you're not an immediate family member, we can't allow you in there right now."

I thanked her, touched Samson's head again, and left the room. As I walked down the busy hallway, I wondered if my attempt at healing had helped Samson at all.

What kind of infection did he have?

I pondered the complicated nature of the creatures that passed through the Veil. They were mythological beasts that existed in human imagination, and they came to earth in the flesh, not as ghosts.

The unicorn that had previously attacked was one member of a species. The Minotaur, whom I had fought, came from a tale about a specific individual who was killed by Theseus. Yet the monster I had encountered appeared to be a generic form of the Minotaur—not the exact one from the myth.

I wondered if the Grendel that attacked Samson was also a generic representation of the monster. In *Beowulf*, there was no mention of infections or poisoning from Grendel's bite. Did this version of the legendary creature return to earth with attributes he didn't have when he was here originally? Was Samson's illness caused by Grendel's magic, or an actual physiological cause? Either way, it was frightening to consider.

In the epic poem, Beowulf killed Grendel by tearing his arm off. I feared that this generic incarnation of Grendel wouldn't die so easily. And here's hoping that his mother wasn't around to exact revenge, like in the poem.

Sophie and I needed a strategy for handling the escaped monsters while I figured out how to fix the Veil. I wouldn't be able to do so if I continually had to play whack-a-mole with all the monsters that escaped.

I realized that even if we destroyed Grendel, it didn't necessarily mean Samson would be cured, even if the malady had been caused by magic.

The only thing clear to me was that I needed to get more of the Goddess's power—for both healing and destroying.

"I'M SORRY ABOUT SAMSON," CORY SAID TO ME AS WE WERE preparing for bed.

He looked wounded. He wanted to support me, but he had long suspected I had a soft spot for Samson. It had developed, of course, while Cory was missing, accidentally sent to the In Between and held captive there by a wizard. For much of the time, I thought he had abandoned me.

After we were reunited, I told Cory the truth: I had been friends with Samson, but nothing ever happened between us. He believed me, but it gave him an insecurity that he successfully hid for years. Until it showed up at times like this.

There was nothing I could say that Cory didn't already know. Yeah, I cared for Samson, but Cory would always be the love of my life. So, I changed the subject to something Cory and I had in common.

"The mold in the utility room is becoming a serious problem." Aren't I romantic?

"I know," Cory said. "I'll call a mitigation company to look at it. They're not cheap, though."

"Would our insurance cover it?"

"I doubt it."

The mom-and-pop-innkeeper talk continued until Cory dozed off, and I went into the bathroom to brush my teeth.

I wasn't the least bit surprised when Birog's face appeared behind mine in the mirror. With a finger covered in rings, she moved her lips aside to check her teeth. They were still black.

"Would you like a toothbrush?" I asked.

"Not funny. Ye know I'm only a ghostie."

"Well, I'm glad you showed up. I need more of the Goddess's power."

I explained my inability to heal Samson. "And even though I fixed the courtyard wall, that's nothing compared to the Veil. I will need a great deal of her power to do that. How can I get more power?"

"Ye're always askin' me questions I can't answer. Only Danu has the answers ye need. As a Druid, I've helped ye connect with her. I've given ye advice. But this is between ye and the Goddess. You need to become one with her—more than ye've been so far."

"I know how to connect with her power. Sometimes, I see her. I don't know how to do more."

"The Goddess will help you when ye're ready."

"How do I become more ready?"

She smiled. "All these questions. I can tell ye one thing, though. If ye want more of Danu in ye, ye'll need to lose the Darla in ye."

"I don't understand."

"More of Danu's power means more of Danu in this world again. More Goddess means less human."

"You're saying I have to be completely possessed by Danu?"

"I'm sayin' ye must *become* Danu."

"I can't be me anymore?"

"Gods and goddesses demand sacrifices. You must be sacrificed to her."

"Forget it. I can't give up my life, my family, my—"

Birog disappeared from the mirror. And I went to bed filled with sadness. It was time to break free from the Goddess and the responsibilities that came with her.

My breath caught when I realized that meant I would be unable to heal Samson. But if I didn't heal him when I tried, could Danu ever heal him? I didn't know.

Perhaps witches could help me. I knew plenty of them. They had magic; I did not. My powers were only on loan from a goddess who wanted to take me over.

From now on, I would stick to my paranormal abilities of psychometry and telepathy. The magic would be up to Sophie and others in the Magic Guild.

This human vessel for a goddess has broken.

I HAD FEARED THE GODDESS WOULD INVADE MY DREAMS THAT night, but she didn't. In fact, the only dream I could remember was a nightmare about mold spreading across the utility room ceiling. Yeah, maybe the Goddess could stop the mold, but I doubted it. The fungi were naturally occurring organisms, and she would have no reason to destroy them.

And it didn't matter. I was done with her, anyway.

Alone in the kitchen before dawn, chopping onions to make frittatas, I turned on the TV for the news. Amid all the fluffy, sugarcoated segments meant to help me start my day in a good mood, there were news stories that dismayed me.

A bar in Old Town, known for loud music and raucous crowds, had been attacked by a "maniac" who smashed windows and tossed patrons around like rag dolls. When the attacker fled, he took a patron with him. She has yet to be found.

Grendel didn't like loud parties. That's why he attacked the mead hall for years until Beowulf stopped him.

And then there was a seemingly unrelated story that took place in China. Wildfires had broken out in an area where this had never happened. Wildfires are becoming more and more common nowadays, but there was one strange detail in this case.

Residents who evacuated their homes claimed a dragon had started the fires. They said they saw it flying overhead, spraying flames on the villages and trees.

The American TV anchorwoman's attitude was one of derision. The unspoken thought was these rural Chinese villagers would believe anything.

I believed it.

Another creature had passed through the Veil, but this one had arrived on the other side of the world. Who knows how many creatures had already done so and hadn't ended up in the news?

Not my problem, I told myself.

Although, I wasn't convinced.

CHAPTER 5

A HIGHER CALLING

Why would a winged angel, who could travel anywhere in the universe instantly, choose to ride in the back seat of an old clunker? That's where Raphael appeared as I drove down Hidalgo Avenue on the way to the store.

His perfect beauty, shimmering with celestial light, clashed with my car's worn interior and stained seats.

"Why are you resisting your mission?" he asked. I assumed he already knew the answer and his question was rhetorical.

I explained I didn't want to lose my identity. I was happy with who I was and had a family I loved. My current life suited me just fine.

"You truly enjoy going to the wholesale store to buy eggs in bulk?"

"Yes. You've got to appreciate the simple routines of life."

"While the lives of everyone on the planet are at risk?"

"Sure, I look selfish when you put it that way."

"The Veil must be repaired, and only the Goddess can do it.

The Goddess needs you to manifest herself in this world and in the semi-material realm where the Veil exists."

"Why can't the Big Guy do it?"

"He created the universe. He doesn't do maintenance on it. That's up to the many gods and goddesses he has engendered. And the repair of the damage inflicted on planets is up to the mortal creatures who caused it."

"What about angels like you?"

"We're guardians and messengers. We don't get our hands dirty."

"I'm surprised you're willing to sit in my dirty car."

A look of irritation crossed his angelic face. Only I could tick off an angel.

"You're not persuading me," I said. "I have a busy life with many responsibilities. There's no time in my schedule to do maintenance on the universe. And why does it have to be me, anyway?"

"The Goddess will reveal why she chose you. As to why the Veil must be repaired immediately, I'll give you a vision of the future if the tear remains."

The angel disappeared from my back seat. My surroundings appeared the same, so I continued driving. The vision he promised would probably come at night in a dream.

I arrived at an intersection, and the traffic light blinked red, as if the power had been disrupted. Coming to a stop, I scanned for traffic coming from the other directions.

No cars. Only a forty-foot-tall humanoid giant lumbering up to the intersection. With a wooden club studded with spikes, he tore out the lines holding the traffic lights and continued on his path. He stopped to smash to pieces a building containing a high-end clothing store.

A flock of harpies flew overhead. The street darkened from

the shadow of a dragon soaring above the harpies. His wingspan covered an entire block. Flames belched from his mouth, obliterating the harpies.

A herd of a dozen unicorns thundered past my car. One of them punctured my front tire with his horn. One unicorn was rare enough, but an entire herd of them? It must have been my lucky day.

My car was now stuck at the intersection, but there was no way I would get out to change my tire. I picked up my cellphone to call for help, but there was no service. Yes, Hell had come to earth.

A loud crunching sound caused me to look up. The spire of a nearby church snapped off, gripped by a giant tentacle. Of course. A kraken in the nearby bay had come up to the seawall to destroy the waterfront area.

Okay, I got the message. If I didn't fix the Veil, driving to the store for eggs would be much more of a chore.

A manticore with its human face, eagle wings, lion's body, and stinger dripping with poison chased a construction worker down the sidewalk beside me.

Until the manticore noticed me. He turned and slammed into my windshield, shattering it. His scorpion-style stinger stabbed at the web of glass, trying to get through to me.

"Raphael!" I shouted. "I've had enough of your vision. I totally get where you're coming from. Please stop it!"

Suddenly, all the monsters were gone, and the city looked normal. The church spire and clothing store were back as if nothing had happened. The light turned green, and I drove ahead, all tires fully inflated.

The angel was in my back seat again.

"You saw only a fraction of how bad it would truly get," he said.

"I saw enough. But I'm still not ready to fix the Veil. I need to learn how to do it."

"You will be taught," he said before disappearing, with a blinding flash of light from his smile.

EVEN WITHOUT MONSTERS COMING THROUGH THE VEIL, buying eggs proved to be more difficult than I had expected. And I don't mean how hard it was to make it past the special displays with the giant boxes of unhealthy treats that neither my family nor an entire inn full of guests could consume before the expiration date.

I made it safely past the stacked cases of household batteries. I hesitated, my living in Florida with hurricane season approaching giving me pause, but forced myself to keep moving. There were already several cases of batteries in the closet from my last visit here.

I did break down and buy Cory a pack of fifteen pairs of underwear. The price was too good to pass up.

The weirdness occurred when I entered the aisles with cases of frozen foods. I opened the glass door to grab a box of 100 frozen mini pizzas, figuring I could serve them as canapés during Wine Hour. As I reached into the freezer, I ended up in a forest.

No, I hadn't passed through a gateway. There was no shimmering air or a feeling of nausea. Instead, I realized, I had been summoned to visit the Goddess.

The setting was the familiar primeval forest with giant moss-covered trees that cloaked everything I saw in shadows. A shushing sound nearby indicated a waterfall. For some reason, I always had visions of the Goddess while she was skinny dipping in the pool beneath the falls.

As I emerged from the trees, I heard her. Danu, the earth mother. The entity who was trying to possess me. She sang the same song that had involuntarily come from my mouth when I tried to heal Samson.

I had to admit, the Goddess could carry a tune better than I.

My feet were at the edge of the creek that flowed from the pool beneath the falls. I stood upon smooth wet rocks in my bare feet. Wait, what had happened to my shoes?

And where was the Goddess? Her voice came from near the falls, but I did not see her standing naked in the pool of water like I usually did in these visions.

I felt compelled to look for her and stepped into the creek. The water was cool, but not at all uncomfortable. It was invigorating.

It was only then that I noticed I was naked. At my age, being naked outdoors was not a preferred activity. But in this dreamlike fugue I was experiencing, it seemed perfectly normal.

I waded along the creek in calf-high water atop sand and stones. When I reached the pool, the depth increased to hip deep. Bear in mind, my hips were a lot closer to the ground than most people's.

The water became turbid as I reached the waterfall. Still, there was no sign of the Goddess, only the sound of her voice.

Suddenly, I realized the song was coming from my mouth. I felt much more powerful than I had the last time I sang. When I was in my human body.

Then, what body was I in now?

The plunging water was so close now that I was showered with spray. I felt compelled to walk into the waterfall, though the force of it seemed daunting. It could knock me off my feet. Even so, I walked into it—

And now, I was in darkness and silence. I felt nothing against my skin. All my senses had shut off. That was when she spoke to me.

Daughter, you must not fail me.

"You ask too much of me," I replied.

It is not I who asks. It is the earth and every creature that lives upon it.

"Look, I'm a mother, too. I know the laying-on-of-guilt tactic to get a kid to obey."

I gave you more of my power when you walked through the waterfall. You are now better equipped for your mission to heal the Veil.

"Why do you say 'heal' instead of 'repair'?"

Because the Veil is a living entity.

"Oh, boy. How do I heal an entity that I don't understand?"

You will understand the Veil better when you encounter it. You will bring with you the faerie priest and an elf.

"An elf? Which elf?"

The one in your guild.

That would be Summer, who was half elf.

The elf and the faerie will have expertise to share to help you with your task.

"How do I even reach the Veil?"

The angels will take you there.

I worried she might tire of my constant questions, but I had one more important one.

"Why me, earth mother? Why did you choose me to be your human vessel?"

I did not choose you. You are my child.

"My mother, Sadie Chesswick, would beg to differ."

You will learn more when you are ready. Go now and perform your healing.

One moment, I was in darkness, cut off from all my senses, and the next, I was overwhelmed with sensory overload.

I stood in a small clearing of the forest, and everything hit me at once with overwhelming power. I saw, heard, smelled, tasted, and touched everything in the forest and the creek—every creature, plant, and mineral. Everything.

I knew where each bird, mammal, and insect was, where it had been, and what would become of it. I smelled and tasted every substance in the creek's water, the drops of dew, the water in the roots, the chlorophyll of every leaf on every tree, as well as the millions of fungi in the soil and on the tree bark.

I heard a cacophony of voices calling to me from every creature, every bit of vegetation. They all were in harmony with the Goddess's song that poured from my lungs.

This entire forest was so alive and vigorous. Even what was dead gave off energy as it decayed and became part of all that was alive.

For the first time, I got an inkling of the true scope and wonder of life. And just think, this power and wonder was spread across the entire globe.

Most of all, I felt at the center of it all. It revolved around me and responded to me.

Mother.

I did not create this life, but I was its mother. Its guardian and caretaker.

Its healer and cleanser.

I realized the Goddess was giving me a taste of what it was like to be her. And it was thrilling.

But I was not yet ready to let go and lose myself to her. I still wanted to be human.

The air of the freezer case was chilling and artificial. I stepped back and closed the glass door, tossing the box of miniature pizzas into my oversized cart.

"They're offering free samples of breakfast tarts," someone said excitedly at the end of the aisle.

This is what I didn't want to give up?

I finally reached the refrigerated cases that held the eggs and dairy. The freshness of the offerings cheered me up a little as I grabbed five dozen eggs.

They were on sale. That brightened my viewpoint even more. I was quickly getting back into my mundane life after my brief experience being an earth-mother goddess. It was easy to do because I'd spent fifty-three years in this mundane life.

As I headed for the checkout lines, impulsively grabbing a ten-pound plastic jug of peanuts, I tried to make sense of choosing the mundane over the divine.

Well, I just renewed our membership at this wholesale club. It would be a crime to give it up now.

CHAPTER 6

JEALOUS DEMON

I wasn't surprised to find my resident gargoyle and vampire playing chess in the inn's kitchen. They weren't supposed to be doing this if there was any chance a guest would see them. But at 3:00 a.m., it should be pretty safe.

"Ah, Lady Darla, what brings you here at such an unusual hour for humans?" Roderick, the vampire, asked.

He stood beside the kitchen counter in the darkened room. On it was a chessboard. Archibald was perched on the subway tile of the backsplash above it.

"I couldn't sleep. I have this uneasy feeling."

"Worries about inn keeping, or something that would trouble only a goddess?" Archibald meant to sound compassionate but came across as snide. Must have been his English accent.

"I don't know what things trouble goddesses," I replied, "but I have this, well, existential dread."

"As far as I know, all is well in San Marcos," Roderick said. "You should be proud of helping to cure the infection that turned this city into a vampire apocalypse."

"I have so much unfinished business. Maybe I'm sensing that another creature escaped through the Veil."

Roderick and Archibald exchanged glances.

"It would be preferable if we didn't have to worry every day about tourists being devoured," Archibald said.

"You don't need to remind me."

Roderick cocked his head. "A vampire is requesting permission to enter the inn. It's Diego, I believe. I'll let him in."

Contrary to popular belief, vampires don't need a human's permission to enter their home. If another vampire lives there, though, an invitation to enter is required. It's a mere matter of courtesy, based on the creatures' territorial natures.

Roderick returned to the kitchen followed by Diego, handsome as always, slim, and statuesque, his ebony skin waxen as if he hadn't fed recently.

"I texted you earlier," he said to me, "but you didn't reply."

I felt for my phone. It wasn't in my sweatpants' pockets.

"I probably left it in my bathroom," I said. "I've had a restless night. What brings you here at this early hour?"

"I needed to get away from the nest." He was dressed in all black, as if he'd been clubbing. "There's an awkward situation with Lethia and the Father of Lies."

Ever since Lethia had taken over as the leader of the vampires' guild, the Clan of the Eternal Night, she'd required Diego to sleep in her mansion instead of his home above his restaurant. She had established a nest in her home for her newly turned followers and wanted Diego to live there, as well. I guess it was an attempt to exert her authority over him.

"The two lovebirds are having a spat?" I asked with snark.

The demon, known to the Fae as Aastacki and to the rest of us as the Father of Lies, was in love with Lethia. He had fallen for her when she was a mortal and brought her back to life as the world's first vampire. She allegedly loved him in return.

"It's a bit messy," Diego said, wringing his hands.

"I'm listening."

"The Father of Lies caught us kissing."

I barked an uncomfortable laugh. "You and Lethia?"

"Yes. It was a perfectly innocent kiss. Aside from a little flirting, nothing is going on between us."

"I thought you disliked Lethia. She took over when you were next in line to lead the Guild."

"Yes. But you know how it goes. I guess I shouldn't have moved into the nest. The problem is that the Father of Lies is not taking this well."

"Didn't Lethia convince him that you and she are not having an affair?"

"He's extremely insecure for a demon. It's made him blow this all out of proportion."

"Are you in danger?"

"Frankly"—he looked around nervously—"yes. He threatened to free all the denizens of Hell and send them here to destroy us and the entire city."

It wasn't an empty threat. The Father of Lies allegedly used his magic to help the rogue faction of Fae tear open the weakened Veil. The Fae had directed the escaping monsters to attack me, so I knew they could be given specific targets.

"Did he say anything about further damaging the Veil?" I asked.

"He said he would rip it open so wide that Hades and his hound wouldn't be able to stop the lowliest entity from escaping."

"Great. Just great. I'm supposed to repair the hole, and he's going to make it even bigger?"

The crash of broken glass came from the nearby living room, accompanied by the slaps of several sets of bare feet running.

"I believe he already has," Archibald said before disappearing from his perch above the counter.

I looked out the kitchen doorway to see a half dozen anthropophagi running toward me. Yes, another species of legendary monsters. These were humanoid, hairy, and naked. They also lacked heads. Their eyes, noses, and mouths were in their torsos. Their razor-sharp teeth were designed to devour human flesh.

"Not you again," I said, before ducking back into the kitchen. This was not the first invasion of the inn by these monsters. And it wouldn't be the first time I needed to replace the windows because of them.

Sophie's magic had been effective at killing the anthropophagi, but she was asleep upstairs, and I didn't have my phone with me. The nearest landline was at the front desk. I called to her telepathically.

"Diego, please call my daughter and tell her to bring her sword to the kitchen," I said, reciting her number in case my telepathy didn't rouse her.

Before he could pull his phone from his pocket, Diego had to stop the anthropophagus at the head of the pack. Moving faster than my eyes could register, he seized the creature and threw it down the hall, knocking the other ones over like bowling pins.

I shut the heavy antique door and bolted it. Doing so risked allowing the monsters to head upstairs to attack my guests, but I needed a moment to harness the Goddess's power.

My human scent kept drawing the anthropophagi, and they crashed against the wooden door. I used the opportunity to force myself into a trance-like state, and Diego called Sophie, though she wasn't answering his call.

The familiar warmth grew in my stomach. This time, it was

painful because I was summoning the Goddess's destructive power. Remember, death is a fundamental part of nature, and I needed to use it to cull from our midst the unnatural creatures that threatened to destroy those of us who belonged on the planet.

An explosive crack rang out as the door splintered vertically. Two anthropophagi pushed the pieces aside just as white lightning shot from my hands, knocking the creatures backward.

But they were still alive. When the Goddess gave me more power, I guess it was for mending, not for rending. I needed Sophie and her sword!

A third monster ran into the kitchen. Before I could shoot it, Diego lunged at it with claws and fangs, and seconds later, the creature lay on the kitchen floor, disemboweled.

"Don't let the Health Department see this," I said.

Diego made another attempt to call Sophie. Roderick, brave as ever, slipped into his crawlspace behind the fridge. And I cleared my mind, summoning more of the Goddess's power.

The first two anthropophagi I had shot were struggling to get to their feet. I had damaged them, but not enough. I shot more lightning at them.

Oops. It looked like this blast had healed instead of hurt them. I seemed to have gotten my divine powers confused.

And now, they and the other three were coming through the broken door.

Diego seized the first one, but the second jumped on his back. Diego struggled to gain control.

Meanwhile, I sent lightning at the next one coming through the door. This time, the warmth inside me was a painful burning. If it hurt me, it would hurt the monster.

And it did. It went flying backward, smoke rising from its hair.

More anthropophagi came at me while my power was depleted. I needed time to replenish it. I darted behind the butcher-block island, grabbing a meat tenderizer, and hammering the closest monster on the head with it. That slowed it down.

But not enough.

Diego had successfully found an artery in one of his two foes, and it dropped to the floor. Now, he struggled with the one still hanging onto his back, slamming it and himself backward against the wall.

He couldn't help me. All I had was the meat tenderizer and the power that was replenishing, but not fast enough. Two anthropophagi scrambled over the island at me.

The top of the first one's torso exploded, splattering the ceiling with goo.

Sophie had arrived! She aimed her sword at the other monster as it dove toward me, sending her purple form of lightning.

Another explosion of monster goo.

In a matter of seconds, Diego finished off his foe and Sophie had turned the last monster into a goo volcano.

"We have a lot of cleaning to do before it's time to make breakfast," I said.

"How did we end up with more anthropophagi?" Sophie asked.

"It's my fault," Diego said, picking monster hair from his fangs. "I made the Father of Lies jealous, and he acted out. He made the hole in the Veil even larger, and he's sending more monsters here to punish all of us."

"What did you do to make him jealous? Wait, don't tell me you hooked up with Lethia."

"I kissed her. That's all."

"Good grief," Sophie said as she slipped her sword into its scabbard. "We have to deal with that demon with the inferiority complex again?"

"Yep," I said. "I must go off and repair the Veil. I can't put it off any longer. Exactly how I'll fix it, I do not know."

I left the kitchen, went down the hall past the living room with its shattered windows, and exited into the courtyard.

In the middle of the starry sky was a jagged line, blacker than black, extending across half of the sky that was in my field of vision above the rooftops.

The tear in the Veil. How could I fix something so cosmically enormous?

The jagged line disappeared. It had been only a visual phenomenon. Yet, the tear in the Veil still existed, unfortunately.

Oh, Goddess, give me the power and the courage to fix it. Please?

A pack of dogs was outside the courtyard wall, barking at the gate to get in. I peered through the narrow gap between the wooden gate and the coquina wall.

It wasn't a pack of dogs. It was one dog with three heads.

Cerberus.

The steel chain that had served as his collar was still looped around the base of the three necks, but the chain leash attached to it had been broken. Only a short segment dangled from the collar.

That idiot war god who dated my daughter had allowed the hellhound to escape. That meant no one was guarding the gates of Hell.

How could things get any worse?

I shouldn't have asked that. I'm sure I'll get my answer sooner than expected.

We spent until dawn cleaning the kitchen. Fortunately, the dead anthropophagi turned into dust, but their goo still left stains. Cory put up plywood to cover the broken windows.

And then, we had to serve breakfast for our guests who had no idea what had happened only hours ago. I wore a fake smile for so long that my face hurt.

It was only once we'd cleaned up after breakfast that I got in touch with the members of my team: a bumbling faerie priest and a cerebral half-elf. Sophie, too, was included. We would meet after Wine Hour to devise a strategy and prepare our expedition to fix the Veil.

It was a daunting task, far greater than the abilities of all of us combined, but that didn't matter. We had to succeed, and we had precious little time in which to do so.

I understood why the team tasked with saving the world was made up of different species. What didn't make sense was that there were only three of us.

Humans were represented by Sophie and me. I was supposed to be acting in the role of a goddess, but, sorry, the last time I checked, I was still human. Wilference would bring knowledge of faerie magic, which had torn the Veil with the help of the Father of Lies. And Summer, the only elf I knew personally, was the wood-speaker of the Memory Guild. She had the ability to draw information from plants and trees, as well as all products made from them.

I figured having elven representation was important because this species was known as the one most closely tied to nature and the health of the earth. Faeries and elves argue over which of their folk have existed longer. But elves actively protect our planet, while faeries have the rapaciousness of humans and put their greed and lust for power over the well-being of nature.

As we sat around a table in the inn's dining room late at night, I laid out this reasoning.

"So, what am I supposed to do?" Sophie asked.

"Guard the home front," I said. "You take care of any monster that slips through the Veil while we're repairing it. Now that the Father of Lies is taking out his revenge on San Marcos, the monsters will most likely come here instead of elsewhere on earth."

"I'll need to stay in touch with you out there—wherever it is you're going."

"The Goddess gave me more powers. I'm not exactly sure what they are yet, but I need to use them to enhance my telepathic abilities so I can communicate with you."

"I don't like the idea of my mom reading my thoughts."

"You're not a teenager anymore. I'm referring to conversations about strategy and tactics."

Sophie shrugged. So far, everything I'd said had been vague and abstract, because I didn't know what we were getting into.

"How will we even get to the Veil?" Wilference asked me.

"I guess angels will take us. How did the Fae get there to tear it open in the first place?"

"From what I was told, Aastacki, whom you call the Father of Lies, transported Jaekeree there so his magic could do the damage."

"Jaekeree's magic was truly strong enough to tear it?"

"With Aastacki's help, of course. But perhaps tearing the Veil was easier than you assume."

"Then, perhaps repairing it will be easier than we think," said Summer. Elves are optimists, from what I hear.

"If only we could be so lucky," I replied. "We don't have a demon to help us, but we have angels on our side. We need some practical assistance."

"What is this talk of angels?" Wilference asked.

"Doesn't the Fae religion have angels? Angels serve God as his attendants, messengers, and intermediaries with humans. Ever since I became a vessel for the Goddess, angels have been visiting me."

"Then Aastacki is an angel of sorts."

"He's a fallen angel. We humans would call him a demon. Our angels are benevolent and look out for us."

The concept of a guardian angel might very well be true because an angel must have been listening to us. In reply to my comment, a shimmering disc appeared in the dining room.

It was a gateway. Most of the time, they took recently departed souls to the In Between to wait for their judgment before sending them to Heaven or Hell. But they also occasionally carried living humans and other creatures to the In Between and elsewhere, even traveling through time.

I ushered my crew toward the gateway. They were reluctant, not having gone through such a portal before.

"Don't be afraid. You might feel some nausea, but it's perfectly safe. The gateway is an angel."

I asked the angel to identify himself.

"I am Lochlor," said a gender-neutral voice in my head.

"Where are you taking us?"

"To Raphael."

Lochlor wasn't a familiar angel name, like Raphael, Michael, Uriel, or Gabriel. He was a lower-ranking angel, which was why he got stuck with transporting us.

"Come on, kiddies, let's get on the barf bus," I said, herding my crew toward the eight-foot-tall shimmering disc. "Just step through and stick together."

Usually, gateways dropped you off—it felt more like dumping you—in the In Between or another location. This time, we found ourselves floating in darkness. Behind us were the stars. In front of us was pure blackness, except for the Veil in front of it.

This is the Veil, said Raphael's voice. He had brought me here once before.

Thick, rope-like strands, horizontal and vertical, were woven in a square grid pattern. With nothing to give me perspective or show how close we were to the Veil, I couldn't tell how big the strands were. Massive, one would assume.

In between the strands was a semi-transparent sheet that appeared organic. Amoeba-like cellular structures were joined together, forming a membrane. As we floated closer to the Veil, it was apparent that the entire structure was thick, as well.

We were moving now, descending, the horizontal strands of the net whizzing by in a blur. And then, we stopped.

This is the tear, Raphael's voice said.

In an immense area, strands both horizontal and vertical were severed and frayed. The membrane tissue between them was missing. The edges of the tear undulated slightly, as if in moving water.

Repairing the Veil will require both structural fixes to the supporting strands and organic healing of the membrane, the angel said. *You will need the magic of your total team, as well as the healing powers of earth mother Danu.*

"You can just call me Darla."

"Are we really here in person at the Veil?" Sophie asked.

No. You are under my spell. I am projecting what you see.

"Do we need to be at the Veil physically to repair it?" Wilference asked. He had reverted to his natural faerie form, which looked kind of like an evil doll.

You must be here psychically.

I couldn't get my head around how the Veil worked to keep evil souls and monsters from escaping Hell. It wasn't as if the monsters were literally floating in space through this opening. But how would we fix it if it was so abstract—like an image of faraway galaxies captured by a space telescope?

"So, we won't wear spacesuits and crawl upon the strands?" I asked.

No. The details will be revealed to you when it is time. He sounded amused or annoyed by my question. I couldn't tell which.

"What do we need to do until then?" Summer asked.

Prepare your magic. Enhance your powers. The time will come soon.

CHAPTER 7
CHILDHOOD MEMORIES

Cervantes had said that something early in my life hinted I was destined to become the human vessel of Danu. It would explain why she had chosen me.

How much can you trust a cat on the matter of human destiny, even if he was a witch's familiar?

Maybe I should go with the next best authority: my mother.

I arrived at Mom's house before her antique shop opened. I used to call the yellow Victorian *our* house, but after my sister and I moved out, and my father passed away, Mom turned it into a hoarder's paradise. It was now officially her house and hers alone.

Except today, Billy Reyna was there, as I assumed he was most mornings. The elderly police detective used to stop by to inquire if any thieves had attempted to fence stolen goods at Mom's shop. Then, his visits evolved into enjoying coffee and Mom's delicious scones—allegedly enchanted with a love spell. Finally, his morning coffee and scones became tête-à-têtes after nights of romance before he went off to work.

"Hey, doll, how ya doin'?" Billy asked when I entered the kitchen and gave Mom a kiss on the cheek.

"Fine, Billy. How are you?"

The kitchen was redolent with the odors of coffee and buttery baked scones.

"Ah, the world's a hard and cruel place," he replied, "but I manage to get by."

He winked at my mother. I didn't understand what she found attractive in the guy with his big nose, thick glasses, and unruly puff of white hair, but he made her happy. That's all that mattered. When they weren't arguing or temporarily breaking up, that is. Both could be charitably described as headstrong.

"Mom, do you still have those boxes of my stuff from when I was a kid? You didn't sell them, did you?"

"They should still be in the attic."

"Mind if I go up there? I'm looking for something."

"Go right ahead, dear."

I told Billy I'd see him later and headed for the stairs just off the foyer. I trudged up the steep wooden staircase, with railings featuring hand-carved spindles. It wasn't easy because Mom had merchandise on some of the steps. What an insurance nightmare. I reached the second floor, where the bedrooms had been turned into display rooms for her inventory of junk.

The third floor was smaller, consisting of Mom's room, a guest room where Sophie had once lived, and a smaller room in one of the home's turrets that Mom called her magic room. It was where she kept her witchcraft paraphernalia and where I once stayed briefly when I first returned to San Marcos and bought the inn.

There was also a door to the staircase leading to the attic. Unlike in my inn, where fake attic doors mysteriously appeared that led you into gateways, this was a genuine attic. It was the old-fashioned kind—not a shallow space above the rafters, but a large, creepy room where you could hide your insane uncle.

I had to climb the dusty steps in near darkness, with only the light filtering in from the soffit vents. At the top was a bare lightbulb that you turned on by pulling a string.

The attic was how I remembered it from years ago: packed to the ceiling with junk. Sagging cardboard boxes, small wooden crates, wardrobe trunks, miscellaneous bric-a-brac on wooden shelves. There was almost enough stuff up here to stock her entire antique shop. She probably didn't remember how much there was.

It took me a while to find my possessions: three cardboard boxes in the corner behind an old standup lamp missing a shade. This was the rare moment when I was glad Mom couldn't bear to throw anything away. For these were the items I couldn't dispose of, even though I had no desire to have them with me at my home.

If you haven't guessed it by now, I was here to use my psychometry. This time, I would search for my own memories, hoping to find clues about the Goddess mystery. I know it was a random, rather desperate approach, but what else could I do? I planned to question Mom as soon as Billy left, but if she knew anything valuable pertaining to the Goddess, she would have told me by now.

The first box I opened contained my collection of Barbie dolls. They weren't in good condition. Don't ask me why a third of them were missing their heads. I guess I was a weird kid. No surprise, since I'm a weird adult.

I spent a good half hour hovering my fingers above the dolls, searching for useful memories. I picked up dozens of stories I had made up about the lives and adventures of each Barbie. When I had played with them, I was lost in a fantasy world.

There were no memories of my little-girl self being visited by a goddess or the ghost of a Druid.

A wooden box within this box contained a small rock collection: crystals, quartz, a geode—nothing valuable. This had been a short-lived hobby, and there were no useful memories inside.

There was a stack of coloring books bound with twine from when I was even younger. I examined a few of the soft-covered books. One featuring cartoon sea creatures had been sloppily colored in with crayon. A book with Disney characters exhibited slightly better coloring skills.

I flipped through the pages and stopped suddenly. A large triskelion had been drawn in gold crayon on an empty portion of a page. This was odd. Had I been exposed to this symbol when I was so young?

The ancient motif of triple spirals was common in Celtic art and jewelry. Some say it symbolized the circle of life.

It was also probably related to the Goddess Danu.

What did it mean that I had drawn it as a child in a coloring book? Had I seen the symbol in a piece of jewelry or an antique vase?

Or had I been visited by Birog or Danu herself?

The door at the bottom of the steps opened.

"Darla? Are you still up here?"

"Yes, Mom. That's why the light is on. Do you have a minute? I have some questions for you."

She climbed up the stairs, still in great physical condition for her age, thank goodness.

When she arrived, she surveyed the piles of junk with a gleam in her eyes as if they were newfound treasure.

"I should go through all this stuff sometime. There could be something valuable up here."

"Doubtful," I said. "These are the things you considered not worth selling, but, for some reason, worth saving."

"Aren't you glad I kept your things? That box there is full of your stuffed animals."

"Yes, thank you." The only stuffed animal I had a true attachment to was my plush dolphin named Doris. I had kept her with me over the years until she literally disintegrated from wear and tear.

"What questions do you have for me?" Mom asked.

"You know that, um, condition I have regarding the Goddess."

She nodded and smiled, as if she were indulging a young child. As a hobbyist witch from a long line of witches, Mom was open and accepting of all things mystical and paranormal. She was perfectly open-minded about my psychometry, and she knew about the vampires, werewolves, and other supernatural creatures in San Marcos.

Nevertheless, she considered my claims of being the human vessel of the Goddess Danu to be a bit of a joke. I had demonstrated very little of my goddess powers to her and tried to play the situation down.

But it was time to get everything out into the open.

"It's coming to a head now, Mom. I have the responsibility to repair the Veil that protects us from the creatures in Hell."

Mom nodded, registering my serious tone, but was not convinced.

"I'm afraid the Goddess will change me," I continued, "that I won't be the person I am anymore."

"Do you need to see a psychiatrist?"

"This is not mental illness. This is about an ancient goddess who has been forgotten by the world and now wants to return to it. And she wants to use me to do it. Do you understand?"

She nodded again.

"I'm trying to find out why she chose me. It might help me understand this better and learn how to deal with it. Cervantes said he believes the Goddess had her eyes on me since I was young. Do you remember anything out of the ordinary from my childhood?"

She chuckled. "You were always out of the ordinary."

"Mom. Please. Did a stranger ever visit me? Did you ever witness me talking to someone who wasn't there?"

She thought for a moment, then shook her head no.

"Do you know what this is?" I asked, showing her my drawing of the triskelion.

"That motif is very popular. I've seen it in lots of items I've sold."

That wasn't helpful. I tried another route.

"How much Irish, or Celtic, blood do I have in me?"

She was surprised by the question. "You have none from my side of the family, but your father's grandparents came from Ireland. I thought you knew that?"

I guess I did. I was just grasping at straws now.

"Thanks, Mom. If you remember anything, please let me know. Even if it's a detail that seems trivial."

She grabbed the floor lamp and carried it down the stairs. Another piece of junk to crowd her shop below.

The third box of mine was filled with forgotten board games. Any memories I found on them would probably only be game-playing details or snippets of conversation with whomever I was playing against. It would be extremely tedious to go through all the boards and game pieces.

Instead, I opened the box with the stuffed animals. Being made with fabrics and cotton stuffing, they wouldn't be optimal conductors of psychic energy. But I checked them out, anyway.

I pulled out a teddy bear missing a glass eye. The fake fur was extremely worn from constant handling. It was from my youngest years, but I didn't remember it well. I removed a pony, a frog, and an elephant.

There was a purple puppy I had been especially fond of. When I clutched it, my hand touched its plastic dog collar and—

—Pablo the Puppy is my hunting dog. Come on, Pablo! I'm on a horsey, and Pablo's running along with my horsey. We're chasing a deer across green hills that don't look anything like around here. Come on, Pablo, the deer's getting away! I have a bow and arrow, but I don't want to shoot the deer. This is weird. Maybe I'm having a dream. I'm the ruler of my people and the Goddess is my mother. And look—boats are coming from way out to sea! This is a weird dream. I just want to play with Pablo. Wait, I hear Mommy coming. Got to pretend I'm napping. Bye, Pablo—

—my little-girl hand let go of the purple puppy, ending the memory.

Wow. It was very rare for me to read my own memories. And this was the first time I ever read one from my childhood, except for minor fragments I've found in my mother's house from time to time.

This memory was confusing, taking place in my little-girl imagination. It was as if my imagination had been hijacked by someone else's memory.

In this memory, I saw myself playing with the stuffed animal in bed. My imagination turned the toy into a real puppy. Perfectly normal.

But then, my imagination placed me on a horse galloping across rolling hills high above an ocean. It looked just like Ireland. And I was wearing primitive clothing made of wool and animal skins. The arrows in my quiver had bronze heads. It was as if I were in the Bronze Age, more than a thousand years before the Common Era.

There's no way my little-girl imagination could have conjured that up. How old had I been at the time? Three? Four? Five?

Like I said, it felt as if the little-girl Darla had been sucked into someone else's memory. Even if I had the ability of psychometry at that age—and I didn't—there wouldn't have been an object in our house old enough to carry that memory.

One that came from the era when Danu was actively worshipped.

What was going on with my brain?

Cervantes was right. My connection with Danu began in my childhood.

But how?

THE ATTIC SUDDENLY FELT EXTREMELY CLAUSTROPHOBIC. Being surrounded by old things and the human memories stored on them was overwhelming for me at times. That's why it was ironic that I, of all people, developed psychometry, when I ran a nearly 300-year-old inn and had a mother with an antique shop.

I left my childhood boxes open, planning to return later to search for more memories. But I brought Pablo the purple puppy with me, careful not to touch his collar where the memories resided. When I got downstairs, I thanked Mom, who was busy with customers, and drove away.

I didn't return to the inn, stopping instead at the hospital to check on Samson.

They told me he was still in the ICU. This time, however,

they allowed me to visit him. I was surprised to find a woman visitor sitting by his bed.

"Hi, I'm Darla, a friend of Michael's."

"I'm Maureen, his daughter."

We shook hands. Maureen was in her thirties and pretty, with a resemblance to her father. He had told me she had two children.

"How is he?" I asked.

"They took him off the ventilator, thank heavens. But he hasn't regained consciousness. They think it's some sort of blood infection but can't identify it."

I couldn't help feeling guilty, even though it wasn't my fault Grendel was back on earth. My guilt made it quite awkward sitting there by Samson's bed with his daughter, in a room filled with the clicks and beeps of so many machines. After a half hour, I said goodbye and left, giving Maureen wishes for her father's speedy recovery.

On my way out, I told a nurse that I believed Samson had received venom of some sort. She either didn't believe me, or it didn't matter.

I vowed to try the Goddess's healing powers on him again but couldn't do it while his daughter was there or too many nurses were around. Instead, I tortured myself with guilt.

Yeah, it looked as if I hadn't lost any of my human, self-doubting nature.

CHAPTER 8

WORKING LUNCH

It felt as if my life had suddenly transformed into that of a corporate middle manager—exactly what I never wanted to be.

We were in a private room at a nearby restaurant, eating salads. In Wilference's case, it was a salad consisting only of onions and croutons with a dressing of ketchup. Don't ask.

I, of all people, stood at the head of the table with a laptop hooked up to a TV on the wall. I was—yes, shoot me now—presenting a PowerPoint™ deck to my team. This was the life I had mistakenly wanted for Sophie: presentations and pie charts and meetings while rocketing up the corporate ladder. Instead, she followed me into the hospitality industry. And into the supernatural industrial complex.

I probably lost you at "PowerPoint deck." Actually, I had only three slides. The first had three bullet points:

- Hone our skills. How?
- Travel to the Veil. How?

- Fix it. How?

The second slide was an illustration I had drawn from memory of the Veil after Raphael had given us a preview of it.

The third slide had only two bullet points:

- Get home. How?
- Ensure the Veil doesn't tear again. How?

We'd been in this room for two hours, finished our salads, had dessert and coffee, and woke Wilference up when he fell asleep. And we still had answered none of the "hows."

"Please read us your notes," I asked Sophie.

"We agreed Wilference would identify the specific Fae magic used to tear the Veil. Ideally, he would use his own magic to counteract the destructive magic."

Wilference smiled and nodded. Then, his eyes shifted back and forth as if he wanted to flee the room and this town immediately.

Sophie continued, "We agreed Summer would use her ability as a wood-speaker to identify what kind of organic material was used to create the strands that supported the Veil and held it together. She would then make recommendations to you, Mom, as to how you would repair them in your role as the Goddess."

Summer nodded. Her long blonde hair didn't look very corporate, but that was okay. I was wearing a vintage Victorian-era dress as I often did when hosting breakfast and tea at the inn. It was my nicest outfit.

"Okay, and then the Goddess has to heal the torn membrane-like material. The stuff that looks like the skin cells I looked at through a microscope in high-school biology class."

"Right," I said. "This is all very logical. How come it sounds too easy to be true?"

"Because it is," Wilference muttered.

"Sophie, please read the last part," I requested.

"I, as the witch, will cast and maintain a protection spell. How I'm going to maintain it from earth, I don't know. But you said you wanted me to stay here to 'hold down the fort.'"

"In case any monsters come pouring out of the opening before we're done repairing it," I explained. "If word spreads through Hell that time's running out for a jailbreak. As for protecting us while we're out there, I also assume Raphael will be our guardian angel."

"Quite a leap of faith, if you pardon the pun," Sophie said.

"I'm the leader of this team," I said. "I'm the only one who can be sarcastic."

Summer said, "In defense of our half-baked plan—"

"It's not half-baked," I protested. "It's a work in progress."

"That's the point I was about to make. There's an adage in the military that no plan survives first contact with the enemy. We'll need to improvise because no one has ever done this before. And we'll need to rely on the Goddess to show us the way."

"That's what worries me," I said. "I can't control her. What if she doesn't show up?"

"She will," Wilference said. "The Goddess Danu will come through. I know she will. Now, can we order more desserts?"

"Who do you think is paying for this lunch? You really believe I can send an expense report to the angels and bill it to a client?"

"I will pay for the Death by Chocolate myself," Wilference said. Then he pulled from his monkish habit a gold coin with the profile of the Faerie Queene on its face.

"Don't worry," I said. "It's on me."

"You forgot to cover Slide Three," Summer said after I placed the dessert order. "This is the shortest PowerPoint deck I've ever had to sit through. I think we can handle one more slide."

"Oh, yeah," I said, clicking to the two bullet points featuring more questions without answers. "How do we get home? I assume an angel will bring us back. After all, they would take us to the Veil in the first place."

"What if they don't?" Wilference asked.

I was about to say, "then we're out of luck," but figured it would be bad for morale.

"Of course, they will," I said with a fake smile.

"No, really," Sophie said. "What if you get sucked into Hell somehow? The angels can't go in there to bring you out."

"We'll stay far from the entrance to Hell. And I can't think of any reason why the angels won't bring us home."

"Just because you can't think of a reason, doesn't mean it won't exist," Wilference muttered.

"What was that Wil?" I challenged. "Couldn't hear you."

"It was nothing."

"What about the last bullet point?" Sophie asked. "Ensuring the Veil doesn't tear again? I hope you're not expecting my magic to protect the Veil forever."

"Well, yes, I was. Being that you're on the team and all."

"Mom, you already know my magic is stronger when I'm on attack. I'm not much for protection spells and wards."

"Maybe you should expand your skill set."

"No, we need to enlist help from the Magic Guild. Arch Mage Bob's powers are back to what they used to be before he was turned into a vampire. And there are witches and wizards in the Guild, more powerful than I, who can construct a spell that would be strong and long-lasting."

"We especially need one that resists magic from those of my kind," Wilference said. "If the Fae can tear it once, they could try to do so again."

"Hopefully not, now that Jaekeree is gone," I said.

"There are still bad actors in the court the Queene doesn't know about. We must continually be on guard."

"There are some who say the Fae are dark elves," Summer said. "The evil opposites of my species."

Wilference frowned. "Don't be a bigot."

"I'm sorry," Summer said. "Thank goodness for cities like San Marcos, where the guilds bring together as allies different species that were once at war."

"And that only strengthens what I was saying," Sophie added. "We've got to enlist the help of all guilds to protect the Veil. Just because it became Danu's project to heal it, it doesn't mean those of us in this room are the only ones who need to maintain it."

"Truer words have never been spoken," Wilference said.

I turned off my laptop. "The presentation has ended."

A familiar disc of shimmering light appeared between the table and the wall with the TV.

"Hello," I said. "Who, may I ask, are you?"

It is me, Lochlor, he said in our minds. *I have come to take you to Raphael. He requests your presence.*

"My second Death by Chocolate hasn't come yet," Wilference whined.

You must not delay.

"Let's go guys. I hope Raphael is not sending us to the Veil already. I need to give instructions to Cory for running the inn while we're gone."

He only wishes to teach you something, Lochlor said.

I herded my reluctant team toward the disc. Their previous experience hadn't made them comfortable with gateways. I'd been through them many times and still found them nauseating.

"What about the bill?" Sophie asked.

I put my credit card on the table with a note saying we'll be right back.

"This is just in case," I said. "We should return before the server stops in. When you travel with the angels, you're usually gone for only a matter of seconds."

I gently pushed my team into the shimmering disc, then stepped through myself.

And landed hard on an immense beach that stretched for as far as the eye could see. The edge of the sea was at least a hundred yards away, and the dunes were just as far. My heart sank as I recognized the landscape.

We were in the In Between.

"Why would Raphael want to come here?" I asked. "Lochlor?"

The gateway had disappeared. I had a bad feeling about this.

"You will not repair the Veil," said a booming voice in the sky. It was the cultured, elderly voice of the Father of Lies.

"Where is Raphael?" I asked.

"Probably playing his harp in Heaven. Lochlor brought you here on my orders."

Lochlor had betrayed us?

"Lochlor has become a fallen angel," the Father of Lies said, as if he'd read my thoughts. "He's on my side now."

"He went to the dark side to get a bump in salary?" Sophie snarked.

"I think he resented being at the bottom of the angel hierarchy and having to give people rides," I said.

"Where are we?" Summer asked fearfully.

"The In Between."

They'd all heard of it, but I was the only member of the team who had been here before.

"We'll be okay," I assured them. "We just need another gateway—I mean, angel—to take us home."

"Lochlor will attack any angel who attempts to come here," the Father of Lies said. "You will not leave alive."

"We had nothing to do with Lethia flirting with Diego," I said. "We don't deserve to be punished for that."

The ground rumbled as if from a minor earthquake. My fat mouth getting me in trouble once again.

"I will destroy you to prevent you from repairing the Veil."

In this utterly barren landscape with the white sky, I easily spotted them: a flock of giant eagles angling down toward us. Only, they weren't eagles.

They were harpies. The same half-birds, half-shrieking women the angels had removed from San Marcos a month ago after they passed through the Veil.

Raphael had said dumping them in the In Between was not the ideal solution. He was right.

The harpies screamed profanity at us as they got closer. How had they learned English?

Sophie drew her sword from beneath the back of the raincoat she was wearing.

"You brought your sword to Chubby's Steakhouse for a lunch meeting?" I asked in disbelief.

"I've begun bringing it with me everywhere. Except for places with metal detectors."

The harpies were so close now, I could see their hideous human faces.

Sophie crouched, aiming her sword at them. Her lips moved

as she said a magical invocation. A halo of purple light surrounded her and her weapon.

Sometimes, the In Between exerted strange effects on magic. I prayed Sophie's would work properly.

Purple lightning shot from her sword and struck the harpy at the point of the V formation. She exploded in a cloud of feathers.

"Nice shot," Wilference said.

Sophie sent more bolts at the monsters. Two exploded in purple flames and dropped to the beach. The remaining harpies broke formation and flew overhead in different directions. Sophie fired again but missed.

"They'll be back," I said. "I'll try to contact an angel to rescue us. First, let's get farther from the water. There's a really big and mean kraken in there."

"This is where you and Cory visited so many times?" Sophie asked.

"Yeah, but not willingly."

We trekked away from the sea and toward the dunes. There were giant killer ghost crabs in the dunes, but on the other side was a rainforest. Lethal creatures lived inside the forest, as well.

In fact, every part of the In Between had creatures that could kill you. What was I thinking?

Once we were twice as far from the water as before, I stopped. The kraken couldn't reach us here, and I didn't believe the ghost crabs would venture this far from their burrows.

"Why are we stopping here?" Sophie asked.

"It's safer, and I need to focus on summoning an angel. Everybody, keep your eyes peeled for any creatures approaching."

While my three team members faced different directions, I

closed my eyes and gathered some of the Goddess's energy to make my request for a gateway more effective.

"Raphael, please rescue us from the In Between. Lochlor betrayed us and stranded us here at the Father of Lies' bidding."

No answer.

I tried calling Gabriel, Michael, and Uriel. Unfortunately, I didn't know any other angels.

None responded to me. I'd never had trouble summoning a gateway before, even from the In Between, after I became the Goddess's daughter.

Was the Father of Lies blocking my communications?

We stood there on the vast, empty beach. The silence was absolute—no wind or crashing of surf. No seabirds called.

I had the terrifying feeling that we would be attacked at any moment. And, sure enough, the ground rumbled as it had when I'd angered the Father of Lies. But this time, it didn't stop.

I struggled to remain on my feet. Sophie, Wilference, and Summer looked at me desperately. I didn't know what to say.

If I were truly a goddess, I wouldn't be stumbling around in panic like the others.

The sand erupted a few yards away. A black, eel-like creature protruded about four feet above the sand. It had no eyes, but must have smelled us, because its head swiveled in our direction.

It opened its jaws, revealing needle-like teeth.

Everyone screamed, including me.

In the past, I'd been rescued from deadly creatures like this in the In Between by magicians who were staying here temporarily. They usually carried a staff that would destroy the creatures.

Today, we were on our own.

A second eel's head popped up nearby. The creatures, with the circumference of a telephone pole, inched from their holes, coming toward us. The earth continued to rumble. More of these creatures were undoubtedly rising to the surface.

Sophie responded quickly, shooting her purple lightning at the sand eels. She might as well have been blowing them kisses. Her magic had no effect.

Wilference waved his hands at the beasts, shouting something in the Fae language. But he was a priest, not a magician. I doubted he had enough basic magic to save us.

My insides grew hot and painful as the Goddess's killing powers activated. My body felt electric as I pointed my fingers at the first eel and sent white bolts of power at it.

The monster didn't even flinch.

A third eel broke through the sand. We were all but surrounded, so we jogged toward the dunes as the rumbling continued beneath us and a fourth eel appeared, blocking our path. All of them were wriggling farther out of the sand.

We dashed through the gap between the third and fourth eels.

"Why isn't our magic working?" Sophie shouted at me.

"I think it's because they aren't real monsters. They're constructed by magic. A magic that's immune to ours."

"If they're not real, can they eat us?"

"Yes."

"So, what do we do?"

"Keep running. And calling out for angels."

The original eels were slithering after us, but they still hadn't fully emerged from their holes. Their bodies seemed endlessly long.

A new one popped out of the sand, dangerously close to us. Sophie swung her sword and my heart filled with hope as the sword easily severed the eel's head.

But the severed body continued to emerge from the hole

toward us. And the detached head was growing a new body.

"I don't like the In Between," Sophie said.

I heard a command in Summer's voice, but in a language I didn't understand. I believed it was Elvish. She had stopped running and was pointing at the eels one by one, issuing her commands.

And one by one, the eels disappeared. First, they collapsed onto the sand, then shrank until they no longer existed.

I waited, panting from my run, until all the eels were gone, and the rumbling had ceased, before I said anything.

"Summer, that was amazing! How did you do that?"

She, too, panted heavily and looked as surprised as I was.

"I'm only a half-elf, and never believed I had elven magic. But something awakened in me just now."

"Almost getting killed can have that effect."

"Elves have the power to create illusions out of thin air, to make objects and creatures that don't really exist but are so realistic-looking they can make a difference. I did the opposite—I removed magic from these creatures because they were illusions and didn't exist."

"What kind of magic created them?" Sophie asked.

"I don't know. It wasn't elven or anything I've seen on earth before. It was ancient and basic, but extremely powerful."

"I believe creatures like this are here in the In Between to get rid of trespassers," I explained. "This place is intended for newly departed souls to rest while they are judged."

"And Aastacki knows how to manipulate these creatures," Wilference said.

"Which means more of them will attack us. But I believe Summer will be our secret weapon."

Screeching came from the sky behind us. The surviving harpies were back.

CHAPTER 9

GODDESS VS. DAY JOB

The harpies weren't magical illusions. They were real monsters, revived into flesh-and-blood bodies after escaping through the Veil into our world, before being transported here. That was why Sophie's magic could kill them.

She gave a warrior's cry and fired a purple bolt from her sword.

It bounced off an invisible shield in front of the half-eagle, half-woman creatures. "Why did my magic stop working?" Sophie asked in disbelief.

"Ye gods! Aastacki is behind this," Wilference said. "He uses surrogates to attack us, but his magic gives them an advantage."

Sophie aimed her sword and sent more bolts of energy at the harpies with the same effect.

"My elf magic can't help us here," Summer said.

Everyone looked at me. Did they really believe the Goddess would save the day?

She sent an idea into my head. I mean, I think it was she,

unless I happened to be more knowledgeable about monster-fighting tactics than I had realized.

I went into my usual trance-like state. The warmth filled my belly and spread throughout my body. But it was her healing, not destructive, power.

Why would the Goddess want to heal the harpies?

They were almost upon us, wind from their beating wings pummeling my head, their old-women faces twisted with rage and hatred. The talons of each bird were extended to seize our flesh.

I sent forth power, not from my fingers, but from my mind and heart.

"Fly away from here. You do not want to attack us," I said in a strong but empathetic voice.

The harpies' descent slowed, their wings beating furiously as they hovered above us. Their human faces were confused.

"Fly away from here. Go to the Veil and pass through back to where you used to dwell. The rest of your kind are there. That is where you belong."

They looked at me intently as they hovered only feet above us, their talons large enough to crush a skull.

"Go," I said. "I command you as a goddess. Go back to where you belong. Now!"

Lo and behold, they flapped their wings, rising into the sky, and flew away over the sea, disappearing before they reached the horizon.

"Is that a new power?" Sophie asked.

"Yeah. I guess it's a combination of empathy and persuasion. I don't think it will work on every creature that tries to eat us, but, hopefully, I can convince creatures to pursue their best interest. Unfortunately, the harpies need a gateway to leave the

In Between, so we'd better get out of here soon in case they can't find one."

We all jumped as a tremendous crack of thunder vibrated through our bones. The solid, plain-white sky crinkled like a sheet of paper. Thunder boomed again, and a breeze coursed across the beach.

Never before had I experienced wind while in the In Between.

"It's a battle of the gods," said Wilference.

"Or between an angel and a demon," said Sophie.

Suddenly, everything went dark. There was no ambient light, so I couldn't even see my hand in front of my face. I felt suspended in nothingness.

I am right beside you, Raphael's voice said in my mind. *Move toward the energy.*

"Did you guys hear that?" I asked.

They murmured yeses.

"Let's all hold hands, and I'll lead you. I can sense the gateway better than you."

I reached blindly until I felt hands. The one to my right was Sophie's. My left hand took Summer's. With shuffling steps, I moved us across the sand toward the energy field I sensed just to our left. The familiar nausea began in my gut.

Hurry, Raphael said.

My senses told me we were right beside the gateway. I stepped forward and jerked the group toward me.

"Um, please take us to Chubby's Steakhouse. I left my credit card and laptop there," I said right before the sensation of falling.

We landed awkwardly in the private dining room. My elbow hit a plate, and Wilference's second dessert went flying onto the floor.

"Sorry," I said. "Too much chocolate is bad for you."

The door opened, and the server appeared.

"Where did you guys go?"

"We stepped out for a breath of air." And attacks from several monsters.

She handed me the processed check and my credit card.

"Oh, your dessert fell on the floor. Let me get you another one."

"That's okay," I said. "We have to—"

"Please get me another one!" Wilference insisted.

I shrugged and sat down to wait. I needed to return to the inn before Teatime.

"So, what did we learn today?" I asked my team, as if they were students.

Sophie raised her hand. "Lochlor is a traitor, a fallen angel. Summer has magic powers we hadn't known about. And Danu has given you an empathetic power of persuasion."

"How can these learnings help us fix the Veil?"

Everyone blinked stupidly.

"Right. I feel the same way. We'll need to improvise a lot when we're sent on our mission."

By nature, I was the kind who rushed headlong into action without proper planning. But with my crew's safety in my hands, and the fate of the entire freaking world on our shoulders, I wished we had detailed marching orders. I guess that was too much of a luxury.

When Wilference got his Death by Chocolate, he offered us bites. We politely declined and watched him devour it in a feeding frenzy. Someone I know will be sleeping off a sugar crash this afternoon.

I WOULD BARELY HAVE TIME TO BAKE A BATCH OF SCONES before Teatime. Cory had been studying my index cards of recipes when I got home.

"Don't worry," I said. "I've got this."

"Where were you guys?"

"I told you we were having a lunch meeting to plan our expedition."

I decided it wasn't worth mentioning the In Between. It would only freak him out.

"Darla, I'm getting fed up. The Esperanza Inn is a family operation. But lately, it seems that it's just me."

"Who is that woman who looks like your wife and is slaving over scones for Teatime?"

"Sorry, I was exaggerating, but you know what I mean. I was okay sharing you with the Memory Guild, but then you somehow put yourself in the center of the Fae invasion. Now, you're an ancient goddess, of all things."

"I'm making her contemporary."

"And I was completely supportive of Sophie learning the craft of magic. But now, she's dating the Fae God of War and running around blowing up monsters. What happened to simply running a quality inn? We're getting good reviews now."

"Only because the review sites take down the mentions of supernatural events."

"Yeah, but we're finally turning a profit. How much are you getting paid to be an earth-mother goddess?"

"You know the answer."

"If you want to pursue being a goddess as a hobby, I'm cool

with that. But your hobby can't interfere with your day job. And I'm not just talking about the hours you spend saving San Marcos and the world. You're putting your life at risk. I don't want to end up a widower running the inn on my own."

He made a good point, so I gave him a hug. When we got married, we talked about buying a bed-and-breakfast. Cory was teaching photography since he couldn't make enough as a photographer, and I worked in an insurance office. Neither of us was happy with our career. Going into business together felt like it would be exciting.

I didn't warn him I would become swept up in supernatural business. Because I didn't know at the time that I would. It was almost as if I decided after we married to join the Special Forces and go on dangerous missions overseas.

Of course, Cory disappeared for a year when he accidentally went into a gateway and ended up in the In Between, where he was held captive by a wizard. I could have thrown that in his face, but I didn't. How noble of me.

"When I go to repair the Veil, I won't be gone for long," I promised.

"How do you know?"

He had me there. "Well, how long could I survive at the edge of existence?"

Cory frowned.

"Okay, let me rephrase that," I said. "This expedition is not like a typical human journey."

"You don't have a clue how long you'll be gone and how dangerous it will be."

"I know. But you have to understand, Cory, that I'm not a normal woman anymore. There's more and more of the Goddess in me. I'm not saying I'm becoming superhuman, just that I can safely do things humans can't."

"Safely? You're sure about that?"

"Um, not really."

"Think about what you're saying. You're becoming more Danu and less Darla. Does that mean I'm losing you?"

I feared he was right about becoming Danu. But I couldn't bear the thought of losing him and others I loved.

"After I complete my mission," I said, "let's go away together. We'll hire a couple of temps, and Sophie can oversee the inn while we go someplace romantic and get pampered."

He didn't seem cheered up by that. "I just don't want to lose you."

The timer dinged. I pulled the cookie sheets of scones from the oven.

"You won't lose me. I promise I'll always be with you."

In one form or another. But I couldn't promise I'd still be Darla.

SHOWING UP AT THE ICU AT 3:00 A.M. MEANT I HAD SAMSON all to myself. Except there were the nurses, of course, but it was a quiet night. When the nurse overseeing Samson ducked out for a moment, I got down to business.

He already looked better than before, but he was still in the ICU. So, I tried to access the new powers Danu had given me.

It was time to take care of unfinished business—things I didn't want to leave hanging when I wasn't certain I'd survive to take care of them. Samson deserved every drop of healing magic I had. While I still had it.

Not sure what to do, I went through the usual ritual of focusing on my solar plexus and drawing the Goddess's power into me. I hoped I didn't have to sing again. Even with all the beeps and whirring going on in here, my song would attract attention.

But then it struck me: surely visitors sang to patients all the time in the hospital. They sang to frightened children or to adults who were comatose. No matter how shut off the patient was, the music could reach them and improve their spirits. To help heal them.

So far, I wasn't doing anything differently. I had my hands on Samson's head while warm energy flowed through my body, into my hands, and into him. Music suddenly filled my head and heart, as it has done before, and I found myself singing the strange song that was becoming so familiar.

Someone stood beside me. A nurse. She was middle-aged like me, with wrinkles in her face that spoke of a hard life but also a penchant for smiling through it all. She smiled sympathetically.

But when our eyes met, something seemed to sync. My vision zoomed into her pupils, and I saw my reflection: a naked Danu standing in the pool beneath the falls.

The nurse began to sing along with me. The exact notes, the exact key, the exact words. I didn't even understand the words, but she sang them along with me.

The power flowing through me surged. I felt as if I might explode from it. And it all flowed through my arms and hands and into Samson.

Somehow, I was taking power from the nurse. She wasn't a goddess, and I felt no supernatural aspect in her. I was harvesting healing energies from this regular person.

It was then that I noticed the song was coming from behind me as well. I didn't want to break eye contact with the nurse beside me, but it sounded like one or even two nurses in the unit had joined in, causing the power to surge even more.

Did they realize what was going on, or had they been mesmerized in some fashion?

Samson's eyes popped open. He recognized me immediately and smiled. Then, I felt an internal click, like a switch had turned off, and the song faded from my mind and my mouth. All was silent except for the beeps and other machine noises.

The nurse broke eye contact with me.

"I came over to compliment you on your voice," she said with a huge grin, "and then he suddenly woke up! I've always believed in the power of music for healing, but I've never seen it work so dramatically."

Two younger nurses came to Samson's bed to check on his miraculous recovery. No nurse showed any sign that they knew they'd been singing along with me.

"Was I unconscious?" Samson asked.

"Yes. The doctors think it was a blood infection," said the middle-aged nurse. "We were afraid we'd lose you."

"It was venom from Grendel," I whispered.

"Oh, right. Now I remember the attack." He dropped his voice to a whisper. "What can we do about him?"

"I'll take care of him."

"Just you?"

"And Danu. She's given me more powers. Quite handy ones."

"Did she heal me?"

I nodded.

"Thank you. Both of you."

CHAPTER 10

PAST LIFE

My childhood memory of riding a horse across green hills far above a purple sea haunted me. It was so vivid I questioned why a young girl in North Florida would have imagined a scene from Ireland like that. I must have seen something similar in a movie.

But when I had experienced the memory—from psychic energy surviving on the stuffed animal's collar—I relived the full experience. I was me as a child, using my imagination to conjure a mind-movie. Yet, my make-believe experience of riding the horse felt to the young Darla like a memory, not simply imagination.

In other words, the childhood me was reliving a memory of an adult riding a horse centuries or millennia earlier. My psychometry had discovered a memory of a memory.

I know I sound crazy. But I was becoming obsessed with finding out where the memory came from.

"You want to go back into that stuffy attic? Why?" Mom asked when I called.

"I want to go through those boxes again and see if I can find more of my childhood memories. I'm trying to find a connection that explains why the Goddess has chosen me."

"Oh, that." She snorted. Though she believed me at face value about Danu, she still didn't fully buy the fact that her daughter, who never excelled in anything, had a goddess in her. "Why don't you take the boxes to your place?"

"Parents are supposed to hang onto the childhood stuff their kids don't want to get rid of, but also don't want to cart about from home to home."

"You have a permanent home now."

"Without enough storage space for those boxes. Look, Mom, you're a hoarder and you have plenty of room in your attic for three boxes."

She sighed. "Okay. Spend all the time you want in the attic."

"Do you have any other things of mine from back then?"

"The nightstands in the guest bedroom are from your old room."

"Oh yes, that's right. Excellent. I'll stop by later."

For the second time, I went through the boxes I had already explored. I had little faith the box with old board games would hold any memories, but I couldn't leave any stone unturned. I pulled out a truly old game called Candy Land. There was also Parcheesi, Monopoly, Risk, and several others. As I had expected, the cards and playing pieces held scant fragmentary memories from me, my sister, and our friends. They were mostly about game strategy.

What's this? Ah, a Rubik's Cube. These 3-D puzzles were big back when I was an early teen. Oddly, this one had been solved, with each of its six sides having squares with the same color. I didn't recall ever being able to solve it, quickly becoming bored. Someone else must have solved this one.

I hovered my hands over it and felt memories of frustration. Why had I bothered to keep it if I wasn't good at it? I pivoted one of the pieces slightly and felt—

—suddenly smarter. It's like I'm possessed by the spirit of a smarter person! I could visualize exactly, several moves ahead, how to rotate the pieces to solve it. This is freaky. I've never been able to get anywhere with this thing. How did I get this insight? As I slide the plastic layers around, the colors of the tiles coming together on each face, music fills my head. I've never heard this song before. It's haunting. I'm beginning to feel disoriented. Like I'm not myself. I mean, I'm still Darla, but a different person in a different time. Whoa, this is getting too—

—weird, that's for sure. The memory ended when the teen Darla put down the Rubik's Cube.

The possibility that I'd been visited, or possessed, by a spirit had to be considered. I don't recall ever having believed that, but re-experiencing these memories suggested that there were more moments like this that I've forgotten now as an adult. Unfortunately, as you get older, you focus too much on all your responsibilities. The years fly by, and you don't have enough introspective moments.

Children, with their active imaginations, coexist in reality and fantasy land. Adolescents try to understand who they are through constant introspection. At that age, I would have been highly vulnerable to the influence of a spirit.

I wished I had more objects to search for memories on. After I repacked the box, I left the attic and stopped in the guest bedroom on the third floor. All the pieces of furniture were antiques, of course, including the twin nightstands I'd had in my bedroom while growing up. That bedroom, by the way, was on the second floor and was now filled with eclectic junk Mom had acquired since then.

The nightstands were dainty, dark-stained oak, each with a

small drawer and a lower shelf. One had books on its shelf about magic. They probably were Sophie's. The drawers were empty.

In my childhood room, the left side of the bed faced the room. The left nightstand held a lamp and was the one I had used more often. In here, they'd been switched around. The one with more scuffs and scratches on it was the one I wanted to examine.

The nightstand had only fragments of memories on it. It made sense because you don't handle your nightstand that much. The drawer held snippets of memories of me placing my diary in there. Trace images of the face of a boy I'd had a crush on flitted through my head when I opened the drawer.

In the bottom of the empty drawer was a word written in pencil on the unfinished wood.

Dagda.

Who or what was that? The boy I'd had a crush on was named Chris. I could find no memories on the nightstand of anyone named Dagda.

I searched for the word on my phone's internet. Dagda was a deity, one of the Tuatha Dé Danann. The Children of Danu. Another page said that Dagda was the son of Danu and the leader of the race she created. A race of god-like humans with supernatural powers, skilled in art, poetry, science, and magic.

Had the spirit of Dagda visited me when I was a kid? It went a long way toward explaining Danu's interest in me.

I went downstairs and found Mom in what used to be the living room. Today, it had the checkout counter and jewelry cases forming an island in a sea of miscellaneous antiques. No customers were in the room, so I felt free to talk. I explained my theory to her.

"Was I visited by spirits, ghosts, or entities like that when I was a kid?"

She thought for a moment, "Not that I know of. You never had any imaginary friends either, but a lot of weirdo friends, especially in high school."

"Does the name Dagda sound familiar?"

"Was that the skinny girl who picked on you in eighth grade?"

"No. That was Darleen. And Dagda was male."

"The name does sound familiar, though. Are these questions related to the Goddess?"

"Yeah. I found a couple of memories that point to a connection to her when I was a kid, but I can't figure it out."

"Oh, I just remembered that I found this for you." She reached in a drawer beneath the jewelry case and removed a small, ornate silver object.

"What is that?" I asked.

"It was your rattle when you were a baby."

"It doesn't look like a baby toy."

"No, it was more of a memento. See, your initials were engraved on it. These were common back in those days."

I took it gently from her. There were memories upon it, but nothing powerful enough to send me into a reverie. I touched it freely, searching. No memories from me. I probably hadn't even touched it.

The memories I did find were from Mom, including the one of her finding it yesterday. Then, there was nothing for decades until a few brief ones of Mom's when she was a new mother, holding her firstborn. A memory of receiving the rattle as a gift from her mother. A memory of holding me in her lap after nursing, shaking the rattle in front of me, trying to get a reaction from—

—how happy I am that you're a girl! I was so convinced that you were a boy, until the doctor told us otherwise. I wonder why I had that

feeling? Your father wanted a son, but I secretly wanted a girl. Why was I thinking you were a boy? Oops, the rattle is making you cry—

—I snapped out of it. I hadn't seen that reverie coming.

"You thought I was going to be a boy?" I asked.

She was surprised. "You read my memory?"

I nodded.

"It meant nothing," she said. "You know how your mind works when you're pregnant."

"Yeah."

"You should speak to the Memory Guild's psychic."

"You're right," I replied. "I don't know why I didn't think of that."

GLORIA SALTER'S PARLOR WAS IN THE MIDDLE OF THE TOURIST district. Her place was classier than most, but you could be forgiven for assuming she was a con artist, like many storefront psychics are.

In her case, she was the real deal. Being a psychometrist, I was among the psychic family, but Gloria did it all. From Tarot Card reading, to clairvoyance, to talking to the dead, the petite, silver-haired woman was your go-to psychic.

After I explained the strange clues I had about my past, she got right to the point.

"Have you considered reincarnation?"

"No, I would rather go to Heaven when I die."

"I mean, have you considered whether you've been reincarnated? The strange memories you believe might be from the influence of a spirit might actually be memories. Memories of a former life."

I was speechless for a few moments. Which was very rare for me.

"Do you think I'm the reincarnation of Dagda, the son of Danu?"

"It would explain why Danu has taken such a liking to you. Especially since you're female."

"My mother said that early in the pregnancy, she was certain I was a boy."

"Perhaps Danu had something to do with switching your chromosomes."

This was all so crazy and overwhelming.

"Would you like a past-life reading?" Gloria asked.

"You can do that?"

"Yes. And it's on the house for you."

"How do you do it?"

"Lie on the couch, close your eyes, relax, clear your mind, and I'll do the rest."

As a psychometrist, I had superb control of my mind. I went into a meditative state quickly.

I had expected Gloria to ask me questions, but she remained silent, sitting in a chair next to the couch. All I heard was my rhythmic, deep breathing. Time slipped by, but I had no sense of how much.

Finally, Gloria spoke. "Interesting."

"What does that mean?"

"Some people have had multiple past lives. You've had only one, and it was thousands of years ago. Very little evidence of it has remained in your psychic footprint. But you were the leader of a people who were gods or demigods. You had a great deal of magic. And I sense a powerful force in your current life that has attached itself to you because of this past life."

"The Goddess?"

"I would assume so."

"What am I to do?" I asked, now tearful. "At first, being the human vessel of a goddess was kind of flattering, to be honest. But it has ruined my life, giving me all these responsibilities I didn't ask for and don't want. I'm afraid the Goddess is going to take me over, and I'll lose myself."

"Has she possessed you at any point?"

"Not completely. Only for brief moments when I'm using her power. But I still know who I am during those moments. I worry, though, that as I'm given tasks that require more power, she'll possess me more."

"Do you want to be free of her?"

"Yes and no. I want to return to my old life. But that life started getting complicated long before the Goddess showed up in me. First, the psychometry. Then, the Memory Guild. Before I knew it, I was deeply involved with the supernatural. There was the Fae invasion. The vampire infection. More and more, I feel as if I need the Goddess to accomplish what I need to do."

"Which is?"

"Save San Marcos. Save the planet. I'm sorry, do I sound like a megalomaniac?"

"Not at all."

"The more I learn about the Goddess," I continued, "the more I believe the world needs her to be active again. Over all these years that she's been dormant, the world has only gotten sicker."

"It sounds as if she agrees. That is why she has come to you to help her return."

"I wish she could return but go off and do her own thing without me."

"If you truly are her child reincarnated, there's no getting rid of her. You know how mothers are."

"I sure do."

CHAPTER 11

YOU HAD ONE JOB

It was just after midnight when my phone rang. It's never good when you get a call that late, especially when you're an innkeeper. Sure enough, the call had been automatically forwarded to my cellphone from the front desk. It was from room 303, one of our haunted rooms. I hoped the call was about a ghost and not a plumbing problem.

"There are all sorts of noises coming from room 305," an irate man said. "A man and woman are arguing really loudly. And there's this banging—wood striking metal—that sounds dangerous."

"I'm sorry that you were disturbed," I said. "I'll take care of it."

"What is it?" Cory asked sleepily. "It better not be a plumbing problem."

"It sounds as if Sophie and Haarg are having an argument."

"Tell them to make war somewhere else."

I threw on clothes, marched into the inn, and went upstairs

to Sophie's room. The argument was clearly audible, even before I reached the door.

They were shouting in the Fae language, which Sophie had picked up while learning magic from Baldric and being courted by Haarg. That meant I couldn't understand a word of what they were saying. I did, however, recognize the sound of him banging a spear against his shield. It intimidated foes but wouldn't work on my daughter.

After I knocked on the door, Sophie answered with a face purple with rage.

"What?"

"You're too loud," I said in a calming voice. "Guests are complaining."

I stepped inside and shut the door. Haarg looked like an Ancient Greek hoplite in his bronze breastplate and shin greaves. He also had, as I anticipated, his shield and a full-length spear. Why, I did not know.

The God of War feared no foe, but when his future mother-in-law glared at him, he gulped.

"You two need to take your bickering elsewhere," I said. "You're disturbing paying guests. And why on earth do you have your spear and shield in here, Haarg?"

"They appear whenever I feel threatened."

"How can you feel threatened by a mortal?"

"Because I was scolding him for losing Cerberus," Sophie said. "All you had to do, Haarg, was return him to Hades. But no, you had to parade the hellhound around in front of all the gods just to humiliate Hades. You and your stupid macho posturing. And what happens? You let Cerberus get away."

"He broke his leash," Haarg said defensively.

"Because you were parading him around. You had one job, and you blew it."

"The hellhound wouldn't have gotten out of Hell in the first place if the Veil had been repaired." He risked a glance at me.

"Don't you dare deflect the blame and try to pin it on me," I said.

"What kind of god would do that?" Sophie taunted.

Anger coursed through Haarg's face. I assumed it was vanity that made him take a human form that was so young and cute, but it wasn't working for him now. He looked more petulant than enraged.

"Are you, a mortal, questioning my honor?"

I needed to step in. "Now, now, Haarg. You need to be humble with your partner."

"Who says I need a partner? I like to go wenching after a battle, but I don't need a henpecking wife."

"Maybe we should just call the whole thing off," Sophie said.

"Everyone, take a time out before you say anything else you'll regret," I advised. "Haarg, can you please help me with any information about what Aastacki is up to?"

My effort to change the subject worked. Haarg seamlessly switched his anger to the Father of Lies.

"That wretched scoundrel. He still hasn't accepted my request for a rematch. I deserve to fight him fair and square without his tricks and deceptions."

"There's a reason we call him the Father of Lies," I said. "Back to my question. Do you have any information on him?"

"He's been betrayed by his vampire girlfriend," he said with a gloating smirk.

"It was only a kiss. But he's vowed revenge on everyone in our city, and I guess, on earth. Do you know anything about his plans?"

Unbeknownst to Haarg, I had been sending him subtle

currents of healing power to stop his anger and make him more cooperative.

"I've heard second-hand that he is gathering an army of demons."

"Demons?" Sophie asked. "Seriously?"

Sophie was getting skilled at blasting monsters, but she'd never fought a demon before. I doubted her magic could defeat one, let alone an army of them.

"That is not good," I said.

"He's going to that extreme just because his girlfriend kissed another vampire?" Sophie asked.

"Aastacki is evil. And vengeful."

"Men," Sophie said, shaking her head.

"Do you know when they're going to attack?" I asked Haarg.

He shrugged and shook his head.

"Are they coming through the hole in the Veil? I mean, demons have come to earth now and then, even when the Veil wasn't torn."

"Powerful demons like Aastacki come and go as they wish," Haarg replied. "Lesser demons have sometimes slipped through the Veil because it has never been completely impenetrable. But now, there's this giant hole—that Aastacki has made even larger." He snorted. "He can bring an entire army of demons through it now."

"Great. Just great."

"We need to fix the Veil right away," Sophie said.

"No kidding. I'll tell the angels about how urgent this is. Thanks for the information, Haarg. I'll leave you two alone now."

I left the room and headed downstairs.

We already know about the demons, Raphael's voice said. *Prepare your team to depart soon.*

"How long will we be gone on the mission?"

To any loved ones, it will feel that you are gone mere minutes. For you and your crew, it could feel like an eternity.

"Thanks for crushing my soul."

Angels cannot crush souls. We honor them.

"You could have fooled me."

"WE MUST BE PREPARED TO LEAVE AT ANY MOMENT," I SAID TO my team. Tonight, we met in the inn's unoccupied dining room. No chocolate distractions this time. "Inform your families and better halves that you might disappear suddenly. To them, your absence will seem very brief while we do our work."

"To them?" Summer asked. "How long will it seem to us?"

"A bit longer."

"How long will it take to accomplish our mission?" asked Wilference, who, as far as I knew, didn't have family members waiting on him.

"We have to repair the Veil quickly. More quickly than we had imagined. I've learned that the Father of Lies is assembling an army of demons to bring to earth through the hole in the Veil. It might already be too late."

"Will demons attack us during our work?" Summer asked, her eyes wide.

"I hope not. I don't know if the Goddess can defend us against demons. We'll need the angels to protect us."

"This mission is looking more and more desperate," Sophie said.

I resisted the urge to snap at her. "It is what it is. Have you all prepared?"

Summer nodded.

"I've conferred with the top mages and priests of our people," Wilference said. "Baldric was among them, though he is allied with you humans. I have a good idea of the magic that Jaekeree used to tear the Veil, and I'm as ready as I can be."

"I've brushed up on my magic," Sophie said. "Arch Mage Bob taught me a new killing spell. I'm confident I can take on anything that comes through the Veil before you're finished repairing it. Except demons. I don't know how to stop them."

Everyone stared at me. In the recent past, I'd delivered blows against the Father of Lies, an extremely powerful demon. But I came nowhere close to defeating him. I believed it would take the full powers of the Goddess to do so. And by defeating a demon, I didn't mean destroy. Only God could do that.

"Let's all rest up," I said. "We could be sent there at any time."

"Should I pack a bag?" Summer asked. It took me a moment to realize she was joking.

"Pack luck. Lots of it."

I gazed at Summer. When I first joined the Memory Guild, I hadn't realized the wood-speaker was half-elf, though her blonde hair and pert facial features would inspire the adjective "elfin." She didn't have wrinkles or any telltale signs of aging like I had, but I was under the impression that Summer wasn't much younger than I. She told me once she was single, with no regrets.

Aside from that, all I knew about her was that she lived in an apartment in Old Town and worked in a small nursery just outside of the city. That made sense for someone as passionate about plants and trees as she. I hadn't worked as closely with Summer as I had with Laurel, the Guild's other psychometrist, so there was much to learn about her.

"Summer, how old were you when you discovered you were a wood-speaker?" I asked.

"Oh, I was just entering adolescence. My father, who gave me my elf blood, regularly took me on hikes in the parks and taught me about trees and nature. As soon as puberty hit, I found out by accident that I could read a tree's history by touching it and communing with it. The same with fallen trees. Daddy took me to a wood-speaker who trained me, and I discovered my ability worked for all kinds of wood—lumber, furniture, even pencils! The same with all kinds of plants."

"Then the Memory Guild found you?"

"Yes. Just like they found you."

"Did you ever imagine you'd end up visiting the Veil?"

She smiled. "Of course not. Though, unlike most people, I'd heard of it. The elves mention it in some of their legends."

"You're the first person I've met of elf ancestry. Are there many elves in Florida?"

"No. We're not as populous as the Fae. That's unfortunate, because while the Fae are destructive, elves work to save the earth. We consider the earth sacred, but don't have an earth-mother deity like you."

"Like her," I said. "I'm just a human."

"No, you're Danu. And you will be even more so soon."

That was what I was having a difficult time accepting. But I didn't think I had a choice in the matter.

I'D KEPT CORY UP TO DATE WITH ALL THAT WAS GOING ON, but I doubted he fully understood the stakes. He hadn't seen the Veil and its damage like I had. I think he believed the Veil was more of a metaphor than a literal barrier that kept the denizens of Hell from escaping.

That's why he slept soundly while I lay awake, humming like a live wire with anxiety. I went into the bathroom and recoiled at my dark-ringed eyes. My face looked more like a zombie's than a goddess's.

"Birog?" I whispered. "Are you around?"

When her image materialized in the mirror, I felt relieved. Normally, she kind of freaked me out, but tonight, I was happy to have a friend.

"I'm scared, Birog."

"Of course, ye are. Ye have the aching in yer gut every warrior has before a battle. 'Tis only natural to be frightened. But we know ye'll make us proud."

"We?"

"The Tuatha Dé Danann. And the Goddess herself."

"I'm completely depending upon her to achieve success," I said. "Because I'm only her vessel, I don't have a clue about how to heal the Veil."

"She'll be with ye because she needs yer brains and yer courage. She'll supply all the magic. But ye've got to let her in."

"Of course, I will. I told you I'm depending upon her."

"All these times when ye've used her powers, it was always Darla, the human, getting help from the Goddess. For this glorious task, ye've got to step aside and let the Goddess take over. Completely take over. Ye must forget your ego and sense of self. Ye called yerself a vessel? That's what ye truly must be."

"Of course."

"When ye're the Goddess, ye won't be afraid anymore."

"But will Darla be gone forever?"

Birog didn't answer. She simply faded away, leaving me staring at my raccoon eyes.

How was I to sleep at all? I turned off the bathroom light and returned to the bedroom.

Where a gorgeous man clothed in white stood in my path, glowing with an interior light.

Raphael.

It is time. Come with me.

TRAVELING TO THE VEIL WAS ALMOST INSTANTANEOUS. Unlike the two occasions when Raphael had shown me the Veil, this time was more intense. It was as if I were actually here. Not my body, but my spiritual essence. It was just like when the Memory Guild members used astral travel to go to our meetings.

Somehow, though, this was different. I felt more present than I did with astral travel. In our meetings, we saw projections of our physical appearances. Here, at the Veil, I couldn't see myself or the others. But I was truly here, and, somehow, had no need to breathe.

Yet, I knew we were capable of dying.

But where was "here"? We were floating at the edge of existence. This wasn't outer space where stars and planets existed. We were beyond the realm of the universe.

We weren't in Heaven. Nor were we in the material world. All I could determine was that we were on the immediate outskirts of Hell, where there was nothing but the Veil.

Basically, we were nowhere.

On this visit, I didn't just see the Veil; I heard its music. A harmonic humming sound came from the giant membrane, as winds coming from I don't know where sifted through the tiny gaps between the membrane and the supporting strands.

Perhaps the winds came from Hell.

An ominous moaning sound issued from the tear, along with the flapping of the torn edges.

A concentrated bubble of energy, glowing red, floated through the opening and passed us. It radiated evil and malevolence.

Sophie, I said telepathically, *an entity has crossed through the Veil. I can't tell what it is because it won't manifest itself until it arrives on earth. Be on the lookout.*

I will.

"Can everyone else hear me?" I asked my crew.

"Yes, I can," said Summer's voice nearby.

"Yes. I am here at your command," said Wilference.

Though I couldn't see them, I sensed them at my side, increasing my confidence.

"Let's take a closer look at the damage," I said.

I stared at the jagged edge of a section of torn membrane and wanted to move closer to it.

Sure enough, I did move, floating toward the membrane as if I were suspended in water.

Now, I had a good view of the end of a severed strand. Up close, it looked less like woven rope and more organic, like a vine. The membrane attached to it contained living cell-like structures that pulsated with life. At its torn edge, the cells appeared dead—pale and dried-out, unlike the purple vibrancy further away from the tear.

"Share your thoughts," I said to my team.

Wilference explained how the Fae magic had done the damage, with help from the Father of Lies. I wasn't a witch, but I understood that the magic worked by traumatically dehydrating the strands and membrane, killing the organic material, and weakening that part of the Veil. The Father of Lies followed up with brute force, slashing the weakened areas.

Summer imparted her knowledge of the organic material to me. It wasn't with crisp scientific language, but more of an emotional, artistic depiction through the eyes of an elf who understood nature better than a human could.

I absorbed the knowledge they gave me, hoping the Goddess could use it. Then, I prepared for her to take over.

No, you cannot heal it from here, Raphael said in my mind. *You must heal it from its other side. That's where the damage was inflicted.*

"The other side?"

Yes. You must do it in Hell.

"I've always been a good girl," I protested to Raphael. "I don't belong in Hell."

That is where the Father of Lies was when he tore the Veil. We angels cannot enter Hell, but a polytheistic deity like yourself can.

"I have a human soul."

You will enter Hell as a goddess, and you will return safely.

"Are you sure?"

Your companions have already been returned to the world.

He was right. I didn't sense them with me anymore.

"You didn't answer my question. What about me?"

Hell is different things for different people, depending upon your religious faith. It is also known as the Shadowlands for those of defunct religions, and it's where their forgotten gods and monsters go. It is where Danu would be, if not for you.

"What if I can't leave after I repair the Veil?"

You will have no problems because you'll just be on the other side of the Veil. You are not descending any deeper into Hell.

I felt pressure behind me, as if Raphael were giving me a little shove. I couldn't believe an angel would push someone into Hell.

I floated forward into the gaping hole. Nothing felt different when I passed through and reached the other side.

But the feeling quickly changed, and I was filled with despair. This wasn't what I had expected Hell to be like.

This was worse.

CHAPTER 12

A HECK OF A PLACE

Hell was not hot. In fact, it was Arctic cold. Though my body wasn't here physically, I sensed the frigid temperature.

It was also silent. I heard no wind on this side, only maddening silence.

I turned my gaze back to the Veil. From this side, the damage looked worse and more of the membrane near the tear appeared to be dying. I had my work cut out for me.

Summoning the Goddess's powers was different here in Hell. There was no warmth in my gut, only in my mind. But whatever worked was fine with me.

"Hello there," said a booming voice that caused the loose flaps of the Veil to quiver. "What brings you to my neck of the woods?"

It was the Father of Lies' voice. It didn't appear in my head like an angel's voice but was audible from actual sound waves.

"Sorry to interrupt you," he said, "but you won't be messing with the Veil. I have other plans for you."

His face appeared before me—not the human form he sometimes used. A bare skull floated in the darkness, with vertical eye sockets pouring forth red light. The top of his skull was pointed, and his jaw was large and distended with fangs like a saber-tooth tiger's.

"Come with me, dearie."

Even though I lacked a body, I felt violently yanked downward. I tried to rise back up, but I went into a free fall like a rock plunging into an abyss.

"Welcome to Hell!" the Father of Lies called down after me.

I screamed, but no sound came out. Even though I wasn't here physically, I felt the g-force of my fall and vertiginous helplessness. Plus, the dread of hitting the ground.

Soon, these feelings left me, and I was floating again.

Floating in nothingness.

In darkness that was darker than black, my senses sensed nothing.

My consciousness was the only thing that existed. I was alone in the vacuum that was omnipresent everywhere before God created the universe.

This was worse than nonexistence because I was experiencing it. It wasn't like I was dead, end of story. Nor was it like being tortured in the fires of Hell or wandering in the twilight of the Shadowlands. It certainly wasn't the joys of Heaven. This was the maddening concept of negation.

There is nothing. There always was nothing. And nothingness will always be.

My soul ached with the realization that everything was meaningless. Nothing mattered. There was no love or hate, wisdom or ignorance, bliss, or pain.

There was nothing but despair.

My brain threatened to fry its circuits as it faced this existential negation.

DING!

What the heck was that? The ringing sound was so familiar.

Was there a light in front of me?

I moved toward it. Yes, it was a solid rectangle of yellow light. I finally realized what it was.

An elevator with doors open.

I entered it. The doors slid closed, and music played. Of course, it was elevator music. Of course, it was an orchestral version of "Hey Jude."

Yep, I truly was in Hell.

The elevator lurched downward. My instinct was to grab the handrail, but, of course, I wasn't here physically.

The elevator stopped, and the doors opened with a ding.

"First Circle," said an electronically generated voice that sounded like the Father of Lies. "Limbo."

I peered out and saw a group of dudes in robes and togas chatting beside a Doric column.

No thanks, I'm not getting off here. I'm good.

The doors closed, and the elevator lurched downward again, stopping with a jolt. The doors opened with another ding.

"Second Circle: Lust."

Through the open doors, I was buffeted by powerful gusts of wind. I hit the "close" button repeatedly before the doors slid shut.

Even I, a mediocre student, recognized that I was passing through the nine circles of Hell from Dante's *Inferno*.

"Third Circle: Gluttony."

Lots of people rolling about in mud and slush in a freezing rain. Not for me.

My forced journey continued, floor after floor, circle after circle. Next came Greed, Wrath, Heresy, Violence, Fraud, and the Ninth Circle, Treachery.

We descended one more floor. When the door opened, the ding had an ominous tone.

"We've now reached the innermost circle of Hell," the automated voice said. "And it's all about you."

I was no longer in the elevator. I was in my childhood room, as it had existed when it was mine and not filled with junk for sale. Lying on the bed was a girl who looked like me at five or six years old. My vantage point of the scene was from the ceiling, as if I were having an out-of-body experience.

The Father of Lies' voice boomed as if from a loudspeaker for all the world to hear.

"This is you when you stole your mother's lipstick, drew on the wall with it, and blamed your little sister. This is but one example of the deceit, selfishness, and treachery that define your life."

The Father of Lies went on to list every bad thing I'd done in my life. I saw them occur, like reenactment videos, making each one feel like a gut punch.

Yes, there were lies and betrayals. Petty rule breaking. Uncalled-for acts of cruelty. They had always seemed minor to me in retrospect, after I had suffered regret and atoned in one way or another.

But as presented by the Father of Lies, and witnessed by me now, my sins appeared to be unforgivable. My acts of atonement had been insufficient. He also eagerly pointed out all the mean things I'd done that I had never atoned for.

Every single act of cruelty I'd performed was spotlighted and played before my eyes. Every human and other living creature I'd harmed in any way was dredged up from forgotten memories and shoved into my face.

I felt like the worst person in the world. It was true that I was selfish and deceitful. I was manipulative and conniving. I was cruel and vindictive.

I was inhuman.

As the Father of Lies systematically broke down my self-esteem, all my other faults were amplified—even the traits that weren't my fault. I was short, not particularly attractive, short-tempered, with a short attention span. I was impulsive and reckless. Plus, I was lazy and stupid. I wasn't very bright. Add to those faults that I was an ungrateful daughter, a terrible wife, and an even worse mother.

In short, I didn't deserve anyone's love.

I didn't even deserve to live. Why had the Goddess chosen such a lousy human being as me?

"Think of your husband," the Father of Lies said, "saddled with running your mismanaged inn while you're on this ridiculous boondoggle you have no business undertaking. The poor man whom you betrayed while he was held captive by the wizard. True, you never committed adultery, but you did in your mind. In your heart. That was just as evil as if you had done it in the flesh."

I whimpered. This was all too much to bear. Leave me alone and let me rot in Hell. I hated myself.

"You've endangered Cory dozens of times while you selfishly embarked on your stupid schemes. Think of all the times he almost lost his life because of you."

This was true, I realized, sobbing. I didn't deserve Cory. Or anyone.

"And because your over-inflated ego believed you could fix the Veil, the latest creature to escape through it traveled directly to your inn. Right to your husband. Endangering your daughter, too. Behold."

A massive griffin—a lion with the head and wings of an eagle—had Cory cornered in our cottage. The beast screeched, its open beak only inches from Cory's face, while Cory shook from fear.

"This is your fault."

The beast attacked and took Cory into its beak.

I screamed and everything went black. My brain shut down. I was done.

SOMETHING WITHIN ME STIRRED, MAKING ME REALIZE I wasn't dead. Still, everything was darkness, and I had no input from any of my senses. I would have preferred to be dead.

Please, make my mind shut off and make me unconscious again.

My brain kept working. It was bothered by a fact I had forgotten. The realization crept into my consciousness slowly.

The Father of Lies received that name for a reason. Why would I trust anything he told me?

But he was right about all the terrible things I'd done. He didn't invent them; they had actually happened. I was horrible.

Still, the memories he had brought to life could have been twisted or slanted. Perhaps these memories were slightly inaccurate and were depicted as worse than they really had been.

With my self-esteem turned to self-loathing, I agreed with this hypothesis intellectually, but didn't agree in my gut. It was as if I wanted to believe the worst about myself.

The nagging part of my brain kept bothering me.

Why was I listening to a demon? He had nothing but ill will toward me. I wasn't perfect—nobody is—but perhaps I wasn't as bad as I now believed I was. I had to have some redeeming qualities, right?

Who cares? My husband was dead while I was in Hell, having failed in my mission.

What if he wasn't really dead, though? The scene I had witnessed of his death could have been an illusion. A deep fake. After all, who was better at deceit than the Father of Lies?

There was no way for me to learn the truth now that I was trapped in Hell. It didn't really matter because my life was over, anyway.

A supernatural presence loomed over me. Had the Father of Lies come to torment me further?

"Please leave me alone," I said into the void.

The feeling persisted. A force probed my mind and my soul. I didn't feel violated, though. The force was warm and caring, akin to my mother checking on me while I was feverish in bed.

Was it the Goddess?

Whoever it was said nothing, but remained with me. Looking inside me, diagnosing me. Assessing my strength and will.

I had been broken by the Father of Lies. The woman formerly known as Darla Chesswick was now merely an empty husk.

A vessel for the Goddess. A container lacking ego and free will. Finally, I understood what she wanted from me.

"Yes," I said. "I am ready. I am nothing without you."

Who knows how the Goddess found me in the innermost circle of Hell? I supposed it was a hell of my own making, engineered by the Father of Lies. All that mattered was the Goddess was here now.

I now knew why she had chosen me. It wasn't just because I

was the reincarnation of her child. It was because I, Darla, was a worthy vessel for her child's spirit and for Danu herself.

Wordlessly, she assured me that the Father of Lies *had* been lying to me, twisting my memories, and making me hate myself. He was breaking my will and sense of self, so I would no longer be a threat to him. So I would not be able to help Danu return to the world. He wanted the Veil to remain torn asunder so monsters could terrorize the earth and act as his agents against his enemies.

Danu made me feel worthy and proud. As well as determined to do what was right.

I felt her seep into me. It wasn't like before, with a warmth beginning in my core. Now, it was her raw, unbridled power entering me.

The power flowed into me now, faster and stronger with every moment. Filling this vessel. Soon, her power gushed like the waterfall I've seen in my visions of her.

Pressure built inside of me. My brain was buzzing like a beehive. Something had to give, and with a pop like a bubble bursting, it did.

I was Danu, earth mother, for real.

At my feet was the Father of Lies, a weak, frightened old man. He looked up at me with panic as his flesh melted away, revealing moldering bones. He scurried away into the darkness like a cockroach.

I didn't have time for him. The Veil needed healing. And I now had, from the faerie and the elf, the knowledge I needed to do so.

My steed nuzzled me in my shoulder blade. His name was Cael. I turned and kissed him on his black muzzle, then leaped upon his bare back. All I wore was a white tunic with a border pattern of triskelions.

We rode through Hell, through all the underworlds: Elysium, Annwn, Naraka, Patala, Jahannam, and the Shadowlands. The god of these places, Hades, dared not catch us, and his hound was still on earth. Cael galloped to the edge of Hell, the border between being and nothingness.

There, the damaged Veil waited for my healing touch.

CHAPTER 13

WON'T GET FOOLED AGAIN

I sat in Mom's kitchen, sipping bitter coffee, smelling her scones baking in the oven. While her scones had included magic that made men fall in love, mine were tastier. My guests constantly raved about them.

Mom stood at the counter, her back to me, working on something I couldn't see.

That's when I realized I had been enchanted. This was an illusion created by the Father of Lies. I had been at the edge of Hell, about to repair the Veil. How had I ended up in Mom's kitchen?

"I applaud you for your power," I said, "but what's the point?"

"Whatever are you talking about, dear?" Mom asked.

It was her voice. But it couldn't be Mom.

"Are you doing this just to prove you can mess with a goddess? You can't stop me from fixing the Veil."

"I think you're taking this goddess fantasy too far," Mom

said. "I allowed you to have your fun, but I'm concerned about you now. It's time for you to see a doctor. This is not healthy."

Imagine if it really had been just a fantasy all this time. My life would be so much simpler if I weren't a goddess.

No, I am the Goddess. I experienced the transformation in which I became her.

"The Goddess has taken me over," I said.

"How could that be? You're speaking to me as Darla now. I hear the doubt in your voice. It could be a multiple personality disorder making you think you're the Goddess now and then. Right now, you're transforming back to your Darla self."

How could that be? I wondered. If the Goddess had fully taken me over, I wouldn't have been deceived by the Father of Lies into thinking I was in Mom's kitchen. He tricked Darla's brain, not the Goddess's.

Or had he? Might I actually be in Mom's kitchen and everything I had gone through in Hell was just a dream?

I stared at my coffee mug. It was white with two sunflowers on the outside. The inside was stained brown from the many years of my coffee consumption, ever since my parents had told me I was old enough to drink it. Mom had kept this mug and served me coffee in it every time I came to visit.

A memory tickled the back of my brain.

Yes, the last time I was here, the mug was missing. Mom had apologized and said it had fallen and broken when she removed it from the dishwasher.

When she had told me this, I'd been preoccupied and hadn't thought much about it. I wasn't so attached to this stained old mug that I would mourn it.

The Father of Lies had missed the recent memory of the broken mug when he plumbed my consciousness to create this false experience. The mug in my hands didn't exist anymore.

Okay, so this *was* all an illusion. He was messing with my mind. But that meant I still had a mind to mess with.

The Goddess hadn't completely erased my human self. I was not only Danu now; I still had Darla in me, though the Goddess might dominate at times.

Maybe, I was Danu-Darla. Danla. Or Darlu. Never mind.

I got up from the kitchen table and walked over to Mom. I held her by her shoulders and turned her around to face me.

She looked like Mom.

"Dear? What are you doing?" she asked.

"Father of Lies, I see through your tricks. Very impressive that you can do this to a goddess, but I don't have time for your nonsense."

Mom's eyes had appeared concerned when I turned her around. Now they narrowed with anger. They weren't her eyes anymore.

"I'm more powerful than you," she said. "You're a forgotten goddess, weak and washed up. I'm the relevant one. I affect humans every day."

"I don't care that you manipulate people. That doesn't make you stronger. My role is to protect and nurture the earth. And the earth needs me now more than ever. No one needs you."

"Humans wouldn't be human if it weren't for me."

He was probably right, but I didn't care.

"Why are you impeding me from repairing the Veil?"

"I first helped the Fae tear it because they wanted mythological monsters to kill you, a goddess," he said in Mom's voice. "Now, I want to punish the vampires and all the creatures of earth for Lethia's treachery."

"That seems beneath you."

Mom's face registered surprise. "What do you mean?"

"As a powerful demon, you don't need monsters to do your killing for you."

"I know. But it's fun. Creating panic is entertaining."

"And you are too majestic to trouble yourself with a lowly vampire like Lethia."

"You're correct. But even a demon can fall in love." Mom looked away.

"Love is beneath you."

"Are you trying to flatter me?" the demon asked.

"No. We both have more important things to do. I am going to repair the Veil. You can't stop me."

"I have so far."

"There are so many other planets in the universe with other creatures you can manipulate. You can make them worship you."

Mom's eyes lit up with the possibility.

At that moment, I knew his hold on my mind was weak enough for me to break free.

I sent a wave of power at him, temporarily paralyzing him.

Which of us was more powerful? That remained to be seen. I was certain, though, that my work was more important than his malign influence on the populations of earth.

I knew I would have to battle the Father of Lies again and ultimately defeat him. But for now, my powers could block him while I proceed with my work.

And I became Danu once more, sitting upon my horse. The Veil stretched in front of me, waiting for my healing touch.

As I'd noted before, the Veil was made of living tissue and fibers. It wasn't sentient, but I sensed it was aware of me and welcomed me.

And I loved it, for it was a living creature created by God. I felt empathy for this non-sentient creature, and the empathy and love triggered a tidal wave of power surging through me.

Along with the power came the familiar notes of my song. It poured from my mouth and filled the void, turning the silence of Hell into a symphony hall.

The Veil was so close I could touch it, but something in my memory told me not to. Instead, I extended my arms toward damaged sections and sent the healing power into them.

Thanks to the knowledge given to me by Summer and Wilference, I wiped away all traces of the Fae magic while mending the fibers of the supporting strands. Then, I healed the membrane, watching cells instantly replicate and the tissue spread.

Before the hole closed completely, I urged my horse to carry us through it to the other side so we wouldn't be trapped in Hell.

When the tear had finally healed, the entire entity quivered and gave off a sound that sounded like a sigh, one that echoed through the universe.

I had one last task. To prevent the Father of Lies from returning here and tearing the Veil again, I applied a layer of magic that would protect the Veil like the bark of a tree. It was much more powerful than any protection spell Sophie could cast.

Good work, Raphael's voice said in my mind. *The angels will guard the Veil. At least on this side. You may return to your human life now.*

"As a human?"

He didn't answer.

I woke up in bed, long before dawn. The clock read 3:12 a.m., only a minute or two after the last time I saw it before I went to the Veil. Cory snored beside me. I shook him awake.

"You're not dead!" I said as I kissed him.

"Thanks for letting me know."

I was about to tell him about the griffin eating him but decided it could wait until morning.

"Sorry," I said. "I had a bad dream."

His snoring resumed, and I quickly fell into the sleep that had eluded me during the anxious hours before I was sent to the Veil.

"SO, YOU DIDN'T GET ATTACKED BY A GRIFFIN?" I ASKED CORY as he brushed his teeth that morning.

"A what?"

"A mythological monster with the body of a lion and the wings and head of an eagle."

"Not that I recall. I got a mosquito bite, though. The little pissant was buzzing my ear until it finally bit me." He scratched a reddened area on his neck. "Why do you ask?"

"The Veil has been repaired."

He looked at me, startled. "Who repaired it?"

"We did. Last night."

"That's fantastic! Congratulations! I'm so proud of you. That means no more anthropophagi invading the inn?"

"Yep. Why are you looking at me like that?"

"There's something different about you. I can't put my finger on it."

Truth was, I felt a bit off. But not as much as I should have. I had become Danu. The Goddess had taken me over above and beyond my ego and personality. So why did I feel like regular Darla, albeit a bit odd?

I explained to Cory my conundrum.

"I'm glad you're still Darla," he said, hugging me. "I wouldn't want to lose you. I didn't know the Goddess wanted to take you over completely."

"It's the only way to use her full power. But I felt like I was her for just a short amount of time when I was repairing the Veil. I was afraid of losing my identity when I became her. Actually, I was afraid I might have to die and be resurrected as Danu. You know, death and rebirth are common themes in religion and mythology."

Cory stroked his chin with concern. "Is that still a danger?"

"I hope not." It hadn't occurred to me that my transformation might still be ongoing. Did I still have to worry about this?

"Well, I'm going to prepare breakfast now. And pretend that life is normal."

"Can't it be normal now? You repaired the Veil, after all."

"Yes, but I can still feel the Goddess in me. And the Father of Lies is still a problem who needs to be dealt with. I was able to brush him aside to complete my work, but, apparently, the Goddess isn't strong enough to put him out of commission. I need to do that, or he'll be a constant threat to the Veil and to all of us in San Marcos and the world."

When I entered the kitchen, Sophie grabbed me in an enormous hug. Believe me, this was a much warmer reception than I get most mornings.

"Mom! You're back already? Is the Veil repaired?"

"Yes. It has been healed. That's the way I prefer to describe it. And I think I was gone for only seconds, even though it felt like hours when I was out there. And in Hell."

"You were in Hell?"

"I took a quick tour. It's as bad as they say. Worse, even. So be good because you don't want to end up there."

"That's amazing."

"Have you come across a griffin? I told you I saw something

come through the Veil before we fixed it, and the Father of Lies depicted it as a griffin that killed Cory. Cory's fine. I should have known the demon was lying."

"I think something did come through the Veil and arrive here; I sensed a disturbance in the supernatural energy. Since then, I've been on alert, but nothing has made an appearance."

I frowned. "Any strange stories on the news this morning?"

"There was one about a drunk man who shoplifted fifty pounds of sausages while naked. But that's not strange for Florida." She studied me. "There's something different about you, Mom."

"I guess it was all the stuff I've been through. And the Goddess."

"I'm glad you're still you."

"So am I."

I was the real me until I suddenly wasn't, right in the middle of making scrambled eggs. One moment, I was stirring them in a large skillet. And the next, I was wearing my tunic, riding Cael up a hillside that had been devastated by a wildfire.

I reached the crest of a hill and surveyed the landscape. It was a sunny day, but the smoke from the smoldering remains of the fire made the view dark and ominous. Hundreds of acres of forest had been burned to the ground.

My heart ached. So many fine trees were lost. So many creatures had lost their homes or been killed.

There were no destroyed homes or signs of humans here. I wasn't sure where I was or in what era. All I knew was that I was here to heal the land.

I dismounted Cael and led him by the bridle as I walked through the blackened landscape. My bare feet felt no pain from the occasional ember I trod upon. My lungs didn't suffer from the lingering smoke I breathed.

I was in full Goddess mode. Thoughts of my life in San Marcos were faint and distant, mingled among my memories of serving for millennia as a deity, taking care of my earth and my creatures.

Walking through the ashes, I awakened tree roots that had survived deep underground. I created green shoots that would soon pop up from below. A soft rain fell at my command, cooling the burned land and extinguishing all the remaining embers. With the moisture, I prepared the soil across the devastated land, mixing in nutrients from the ashes to support life again.

Some creatures had left eggs buried, and these I blessed and ensured they would survive to hatch when conditions were right. I scattered seeds and spores. I prayed for the animals that had perished, and called to those who'd escaped, encouraging them to return as soon as food appeared.

Nature endures and can rise again after the worst disasters, even those caused by civilization. This is because of me, Danu, and my love—and the creator's love—of the earth.

The smell of rain and soil and smoke transformed into a different burning.

"You're overcooking the eggs." Sophie frowned at me.

"What?"

"Mom, snap out of it! We have to throw out those eggs and start over."

I looked down at the skillet with its singed scrambled eggs and yanked it off the burner.

"I had a moment," I explained. "I wasn't here anymore and was the Goddess. Not a senior moment. A Goddess moment."

"You'd think a goddess would be a better cook."

"I was healing the land after a wildfire."

"That's all well and good, Mom, but can you do your healing after breakfast next time?"

CHAPTER 14
FROZEN

I made it through the rest of the day without incident until Wine Hour. According to Cory, I was pouring cabernet for a guest as we stood in the foyer. I held the bottle above the glass in her outstretched hand and executed a perfect pour.

Until I froze like a deer in headlights.

According to Cory, I stood like a statue, eyes focused on some faraway place, while the wine kept pouring. And pouring. And overflowing from the guest's glass.

Cory and the guest called out to me, but I didn't hear. The guest pulled her glass away and attempted to grab the bottle from me, but I wouldn't let go. She tried to tilt it upright, but I was too strong to budge.

Cory rushed over to me and tried to wrest the bottle from my grasp. He had as much luck as the guest had. The bottle was now empty, with an enormous puddle of expensive wine on the floor, and the half dozen guests in attendance were staring at me in horror.

According to Cory, I remained frozen for nearly a minute

longer.

I should say, it was my body that was frozen. I, as Danu, was on the bank of a flooded river, coaxing a stream to branch out through the mud and take some of the swollen river's water elsewhere. It seemed kind of ironic when I saw the puddle of wine.

"Oh, dang," I said. "How did I spill all this wine?"

"You froze," Cory said. "Sophie said you did it this morning, too, while cooking eggs."

I shook my head with embarrassment.

"I'm a physician," the guest with the overly generous pour said. "You should see a neurologist. You might be experiencing mild seizures."

"Thank you. We'll do that," Cory said.

I nodded, my face still red.

What I couldn't say was that I had frozen because I had gone away. I had become the Goddess, leaving the empty shell of Darla unattended.

"I'm worried about you," Cory said to me as we cleaned up.

"Losing me for a minute here and there is much better than losing me entirely to Danu."

He frowned when I said her name.

THE NEXT TIME I LEFT MY BODY BEHIND, IT WAS IN THE middle of the night when I was in bed. No worries about freaking anyone out by freezing.

However, the incident was concerning for another reason. The protective magic with which I had covered the Veil had been disturbed. It caused me to become the Goddess and check out what was going on.

As I had suspected, the Father of Lies was tinkering with the Veil from Hell, looking for weaknesses. His threat to bring an army of demons through had been negated when I repaired the Veil, which was a reason for him to tear it again.

Even with Danu's magic, it was very difficult to protect a barrier as massive as the Veil from someone who wanted to breach it. Someone as powerful as this upper-level demon.

The angels were supposed to be an extra layer of security for the Veil, but obviously, they weren't enough.

And that was the problem: the Father of Lies was too powerful. I doubted that I, Danu, could destroy him. If we fought outright, we'd probably end up in a draw, like when he fought Haarg. Though, in that match, the Father of Lies clearly had the upper hand.

I needed to defeat him before he damaged the Veil again or created additional mayhem, such as the spell that had made all the vampires in San Marcos go insane.

The Father of Lies must have a weakness I could exploit. I didn't know where else to start than someone who knew him best, at least recently. That was Lethia, the mortal he had loved and brought back from death.

The one who wounded his vanity and made him lust for revenge against her and all of us.

"I'm going for a little walk," I told Cory after dinner.

"Can I go with you? I don't want you to freeze up while crossing the street."

How do I explain my way out of this?

"I just need a little time to clear my head and understand my role as the Goddess. Like I told you after the Wine Hour, I'm freezing because I'm switching to the Goddess's point of view. Hopefully, I can learn how to transition more smoothly."

"Can't you just tell the Goddess to take a hike?"

"No. It's far too late for that now."

"Okay. Go ahead, take your walk. But please don't be late."

Yeah, telling him I was going to visit a vampire nest would not go over well.

Now, the question was, should I visit Lethia as Danu or Darla? Danu would command greater respect and would not be in danger of having her neck punctured. I would also get there a lot quicker.

If I went as Darla, though, Diego would relate better to me. And Lethia owed me a huge favor for finding her daughter.

I decided to go as my mortal self. If Danu wanted to take over, she was welcome to.

After Pedro, the former Duke of the Clan of the Eternal Night, was destroyed, Lethia had taken over as leader of the vampires. She had also planned to take over his estate on the river just outside of town. Until she found out he still had a huge mortgage on the property. Not all fantastically rich vampires are what they seem.

Now Lethia, her little girl, Yena, and Diego lived in a historic mansion not far from my inn, along with a handful of hangers-on. It took me mere minutes to walk there. Tonight, it seemed convenient; otherwise, I wasn't thrilled to have a vampire nest so near my guests.

I immediately sensed a vampire lurking on the front stoop of the brick Federal-style home.

"I'm a good friend of Lethia and Diego," I announced as I reached the steps. "I'm under their protection, so banish from your mind any thoughts of snacking."

The woman laughed with a low growl.

"Lucky you," she said. "They just got back from hunting. You're welcome to enter our home."

I ascended the steps and walked past the vampire. I could

sense her sniffing me. As I entered the parlor, I heard a television blaring from a living room in the back. I passed through the kitchen, empty of food, and found Lethia and Diego sprawled on the couch watching a movie on a large-screen TV. Yena sat on a chair nearby, engrossed with a tablet.

They looked like any modern human family, except they were flushed from their recent meal and had droplets of blood on their clothes.

"Hi," I said. "The vampire out front said I could come in."

"Yes. I heard," said Lethia blithely.

Diego jumped from the couch and was beside me, hugging me, in a fraction of a second.

"Congratulations on repairing the Veil," he said. "You're the talk of all the guilds."

"It was Danu's healing powers, with the help of Summer and Wilference, that did it."

Lethia looked away, bored, and changed the TV channel. She had a cold, distant beauty, with long red hair and, of course, the palest of complexions.

I didn't know the polite way to approach the reason I was here, so I jumped right in.

"Is the Father of Lies still angry with you guys?"

Lethia glared at me. Diego looked uncomfortable.

"I renewed my pledge of love and devotion to him," Lethia said with a hint of sarcasm.

"Did he believe you?" The Father of Lies supposedly was an expert at recognizing lies from others.

"I couched my words in such a way that I technically wasn't lying. Demons aren't too good at picking up on the subtleties of people's emotions."

So, it was true. There was chemistry between her and Diego.

"Has he changed his mind about killing everyone?"

"He still wants to kill me," Diego said. "With the Veil repaired, hopefully, he's dropped his plans to send legions of demons and monsters here."

"That's what I came to talk to you about. Danu isn't powerful enough to prevent him from tearing the Veil again if he really wants to. We need to stop him."

Yena screeched and threw her tablet at her mother. She'd been cured of the affliction that had made her a veritable monster, but being a toddler for eternity, she wasn't exactly easy.

"I have plenty of more pressing matters," Lethia said.

Was she no longer grateful to me for finding Yena for her? She should also despise the Father of Lies for leading her to believe her child was dead while hiding her for centuries. I had assumed Lethia had been pretending to love the demon as a ploy to convince him to break the spell that infected the vampires of San Marcos.

Why was she still pretending? She couldn't really love him, could she?

Lethia scooped up Yena, who was sliding into a tantrum, and left the room. Diego gave me a hapless shrug.

"May I speak with you for a moment in private about the Memory Guild?" I asked him.

He nodded. We had to leave the house and walk halfway down the block to be out of the range of Lethia's hearing.

"The truth is, I wanted to ask you about Lethia and the Father of Lies," I said. "Why doesn't she dump him? Are you in love with Lethia?"

Diego grimaced. "I am. When I was next in line for the leadership of the vampires, I thought we would battle over it, but I fell for her."

"Does she feel the same about you?"

"I don't know. At times, I believe she does. Then, an hour

later, she panders to the demon. I hope she's appeasing him only out of fear of angering him. You saw what happened after an innocent kiss."

"Was it entirely innocent?"

Diego chuckled. "Not on my part."

"The Father of Lies must be neutralized. We can't kill him, but he can't be allowed to damage the Veil again. For a superpowerful demon, he has a touch of insecurity, believing that his love for Lethia is unrequited. I was hoping to use that weakness against him once again. But I would need Lethia to cooperate."

"Perhaps there are other ways to capitalize on his insecurity. Lethia didn't cause him to become that way. He must have already lost some of his confidence, which made him vulnerable to her."

"He was a fallen angel," I said. "What if he wasn't one of those who rebelled against God, but got booted out of Heaven for another reason?"

Diego cocked his eyebrows. "That could certainly make him insecure."

"Yeah. Rejected by the cool kids. Even if he's a big shot as a demon, being cast out has got to sting. How can we use that to our advantage?"

"You, not we. Remember, the Father of Lies wants to harm me. I plan to keep a low profile for the time being."

"Right," I said. "It's up to me to defeat him, even though you'll benefit when he's out of the way."

"You are a goddess. I'm but a lowly vampire. Dealing with demons and angels is beyond my pay grade."

Angels. Yes, I should get them to help me. It was a demonic matter, after all.

First, I wanted to do some research so I could pretend to

know what I was talking about. Rather than waste time on the internet, I paid a visit to a historian the next day.

Prior to my arrival, Dr. Noordlun, director of the Memory Guild, had done the preliminary research I had requested. He smiled through his biblical white beard, when I entered his office at the college, and stood up behind his book-covered desk.

"Word has gotten around in the supernatural community that you healed the Veil," he said. "My congratulations. Please have a seat."

I sat across from him, thanking him and sharing credit for the mission with Summer and Wilference.

"Are you . . . um, how much of the Goddess . . . I'm not quite sure how to ask this."

"Am I Darla or Danu—is that what you're asking?"

He nodded.

"I had thought Darla would be subsumed into Danu. But I'm still here. Maybe, she needs me for my driver's license and bank account. Before, I would occasionally see her in a vision, and I could use some of her power to heal or destroy things. Now, she completely takes me over without warning."

"Do you physically change?"

"It seems I leave my body and become Danu somewhere else, doing whatever she needs to do, like healing a forest after a wildfire. I'm only gone for a minute or so, but I—Darla—freeze up while I'm off being Danu. I just stand there like a statue, unresponsive."

"That sounds like an absence seizure, or a petit mal seizure. You should see a neurologist."

"You're not the first to suggest that."

He gestured at the books piled on his desk. "You asked about fallen angels and if some were not part of Lucifer's rebellion. Well, I'm no religious scholar, but I found a great deal of interesting material in some ancient Hebrew texts. Particularly the *Book of Enoch*, which is about the grandfather of Noah."

I'd never heard of it.

"There were angels called The Watchers," he continued, "who developed an obsession with human women. They taught the humans forbidden knowledge and tried to set up their own religion. They also fathered children with the humans, a race of giants or monsters called Nephilim, who are sometimes referred to as children of Cain."

"Could the Father of Lies be a Watcher?" I asked. "He fell in love with at least one woman, Lethia, when she was human."

"That's exactly what I was thinking. The Watchers were punished and sent down to Hell with all the other fallen angels. Later, the Great Flood supposedly wiped out the Nephilim. You said you learned the gateways are angels. I'm surprised they didn't tell you if this theory is true."

"I've worked with Raphael to fix the Veil."

"The texts say that Raphael himself punished one of the top Watchers."

"He's not exactly communicative with me."

"You should ask him about The Watchers. But before you do, tell me about your plans for The Memory Guild."

"What do you mean?"

"Will you remain a member? It sounds like your role as Danu will become a priority."

"I would like to stay with the Guild. I love you guys. I just don't know what Danu has in store for me and how much time I'll spend having seizures." I smiled grimly. "If you need more help through psychometry than Laurel can provide, I'll be here for you."

"It's good to know. And do tell me what you learn from the angels about the Father of Lies."

CHAPTER 15

THE WATCHERS

When I got home, I called for a gateway. Now that I'm a goddess, it's a lot easier to summon them. Previously, they showed up whenever they wanted, often at inopportune times. Just ask Cory, who had thought he was opening a closet and ended up stranded in the In Between while I believed he had deserted me.

Anyway, you don't raise your arm and whistle like hailing a cab in New York City. You don't use an app like requesting a ride-share car. You go deep inside yourself and say, "Angel, please."

Well, I could do that because I'm a deity. It probably won't work for you.

I waited longer than expected, but eventually the giant, transparent shimmering disc appeared in the inn's kitchen.

"And who are you?" I asked.

I am Kushiel, a voice said in my head. Another angel name I had never heard of.

"Nice to meet you. Please take me to Raphael."

He does not wish to be bothered by any humans right now.

"I'm not a human. I'm a goddess. Pay no attention to the human body I'm occupying."

Raphael is busy with a crisis.

"So am I. I just have a question or two to ask him. I might even help him with his crisis."

Kushiel didn't answer. Finally, he said, *Raphael will see you now.*

Instead of me being transported to Heaven, the top of a cloud, or wherever angels hang out, Raphael came to me. He appeared on a stool beside the butcher-block island, sitting stiffly with his hands clasped in his lap. His expression was dour, but he nevertheless radiated beauty.

"Hi there," I said. "We need to do something about the Father of Lies. I'm afraid he'll tear the Veil again."

Raphael sighed with exasperation and rubbed his eyes, a surprisingly human action.

"We're having a celestial crisis," he said aloud. "It's more important than the Veil right now."

"Do you realize how much trouble I went through to fix it?"

"Yes, I do, and I'm grateful. We're all grateful. The Big Guy, too."

"Can you tell me about your crisis?"

"You saw what happened with Lochlor. There have been many attempts to get angels to defect to the other side. We don't know if it's being directed by Lucifer himself, or if a particular faction of demons is behind it."

"Why would an angel *want* to fall? Everyone knows what happened to the original fallen angels. I've been to Hell, and, believe me, it's not a nice place, even for demons."

"They are being tempted by earthly pleasures. With sins of

the flesh and other delights of mortals. Angels should have no interest in such shallow rewards."

"The Watchers," I said.

"How did you hear of them?"

"*The Book of Enoch.*"

"Ah, Enoch. What a character, that guy. Anyway, The Watchers were eliminated thousands of years ago. I bound one of their leaders, Azazel, in the desert, where he was imprisoned until his destruction."

"What if they're back? The temptations you say they're using to recruit angels are exactly what got The Watchers in trouble. Newly fallen angels could be reviving their cabal, led by one or more of the original ones."

"Whatever they call themselves, they must be defeated," Raphael said forcefully.

"Was the Father of Lies a Watcher before he was destroyed and became a demon?"

Raphael looked at me strangely. "He was."

"Could he be behind this plot to make angels fall?"

"He could be. We've considered that possibility, but there are plenty of other powerful demons who might be involved."

"The Father of Lies has powers of persuasion that few demons could match. He would make a great recruiter."

"You want Michael and me to fight him, so he won't damage the Veil?"

"The thought crossed my mind. While I was trying to figure out how to stop him, I hoped to find a weakness. His insecurity about being loved by Lethia wasn't convincing enough. I wondered if he'd experienced a more significant rejection, like getting kicked out of Heaven. That's why, when I learned about The Watchers, it occurred to me that he might have been one of them. But The Watchers willingly became fallen angels."

"That is correct."

"His love for Lethia, which began before she was a vampire, proves he is obsessed with humans, like The Watchers were. Do you know if he consorted with other human women?"

"I do not. But I assume so. The Watchers were quite promiscuous."

"Did he have any children with them? Any Nephilim?"

"If he was like the other Watchers, he probably did."

I thought about this for a while.

"What were the Nephilim like?" I asked. "All I know is that they were called giants."

"They were larger than humans, savage, and strong. They were demonic even when they were alive, before they were destroyed and became actual demons. In short, they were monsters, being the unnatural result of divine beings mating with lowly humans."

"Hey, no insults."

"I mean you no insult. You are not a lowly human. Not anymore."

I still felt insulted.

"Were all Nephilim killed in the Great Flood?"

"You ask so many questions. At first, we believed they had been, like all the other creatures of the earth not saved by the Ark. But it turns out some creatures survived in faraway parts of the earth where the flooding was not as deep. It is believed that some Nephilim were driven away by human societies before the Flood and wandered the earth. And it is believed that one or two survived and lived for hundreds of years. Of course, none are alive today."

"If those who survived the Flood became legendary monsters in the culture of the people where they lived, they could return to earth today."

"What are you talking about?" Raphael asked.

"The monsters that escape Hell through the Veil have been coming here as physical beings."

"Worry not, you healed the Veil. Though I see why you are so concerned about it tearing again."

A theory had popped into my mind, and as crazy as it seemed, my gut was telling me it was correct. Or maybe it was the Goddess telling me.

"I'm worried about a monster who has already escaped here," I said.

"Again, you make no sense."

"Grendel is still out there. He comes from Northern European heritage—far from the Biblical Middle East. I believe he is a descendent of a Nephilim who migrated up there and survived the Flood. In the saga *Beowulf*, Grendel is said to be descended from Cain, and in some texts, the same is said of the Nephilim."

"You imagine a coincidence too great to be possible."

"No. The Father of Lies was partly responsible for tearing the Veil in the first place, and he's been instrumental in sending the monsters here. He wanted Grendel to kill me, but Detective Samson got in the way. Grendel attacks noisy places with large social gatherings. Why would he come to our mellow inn if not to kill me?"

"Why would he send a descendent of Nephilim to kill you?"

"I think the Father of Lies wants to re-establish the society The Watchers had created before they were destroyed. Their human women and their Nephilim children worshipping The Watchers as gods. He's recruiting additional fallen angels to become the new Watchers. And he wants to begin with Nephilim from the original society."

Raphael nodded slowly. "I cannot say you are incorrect."

I wondered if Grendel was descended from a Nephilim that was the Father of Lies' own child. I mentioned the possibility to Raphael.

"Grendel's mother, immortalized in *Beowulf*, could very well be the Father of Lies' daughter," I said. "And as a legendary monster, she could return to the earth through the Veil like Grendel."

I remembered that when we had arrived at the Veil, I had seen a pod of energy, an entity, passing through the tear on its way to earth. When the Father of Lies tortured me with false visions, I had assumed the creature I had seen was the griffin attacking Cory. But Cory hadn't been attacked. No one had seen a griffin.

What if that creature was Grendel's mother? What if she was the Father of Lies' daughter?

"I would not be surprised if the Father of Lies brought his own Nephilim back from Hell," Raphael said solemnly.

Oh boy.

"At least with the Veil repaired, more of the original Nephilim won't be able to return to earth," I said.

"It doesn't matter. The newly fallen angels—the new Watchers—will create their own in time."

"How do we stop them?"

"As we did so long ago, the angels must destroy The Watchers and any Nephilim they have created," Raphael replied. "We can't allow a false religion to be established. We need to locate this society and launch the final battle against them. You and your daughter must rid the earth of Grendel. Then, you must assist us in finding the community where The Watchers are living with humans."

I had thought my job was done when I repaired the Veil. Silly me.

It was almost Teatime, so I trudged to the kitchen, weighed down by my responsibilities. Sophie had news that cheered me up.

"I broke up with Haarg," she said as she prepared the finger sandwiches.

"You did?" I tried unsuccessfully to hide my relief. "I hope you're okay."

"I can tell you're happy, Mom. But I don't blame you. You'd told me that mortals who marry gods often meet a sorry end. And I've realized that would be the case for me if I devoted my life to Haarg. He's selfish, self-centered, and an egomaniac."

"Gods don't tend to be humble."

"You're humble, Mom. At least in your human form."

"Because I spent my entire life as a human before the Goddess entered me. It gives me perspective."

"And being a war god made Haarg simply insufferable. He was always trying to pick a fight, always obsessed with being the winner. We couldn't even play a video game without him sulking if I beat him. Then, he'd want to keep playing until I would just let him win."

"It shows intelligence and maturity that you made this decision," I said. "Also, it would have bankrupted us to pay for a wedding fit for a god. When you meet the right man, we'll give you one fit for a princess."

"I don't know if I want to marry a man."

"Whatever gender—"

"I don't want to marry a human at all. How about an angel?"

Before, I would have told her that angels don't marry. But now I knew about The Watchers.

"What are you talking about?" I asked warily.

"It seems I have caught the eye of an angel. He visited me twice yesterday. He's so hot!"

"No, no, no."

"What's wrong with hanging out with an angel? Raphael visits you all the time."

"He's a strategic partner. He's not trying to seduce me."

I told her all about The Watchers and the threat of them returning.

"Angels are asexual," I said. "If this one is making moves on you, it means he's a fallen angel. He's bad news and wants to create monster children with you. Stay away. The angels will destroy him."

Sophie turned pale.

"Nothing happened between you two, I hope?" I asked.

She shook her head. "No. But I was tempted. He's so dreamy."

"He's evil. Tell him not to visit you anymore."

"Okay. I'm glad you warned me."

"I'm afraid life isn't going to get any easier for us after repairing the Veil. We need to get rid of Grendel and possibly his mother, too. And we have to help the angels find where the new Watchers are settling down with humans."

"Can we hire some extra staff at the inn?"

"Unfortunately, no. We're not bringing in enough revenue. We'll have to continue working two jobs: running an inn and fighting evil."

Little did I know that we'd be fighting evil later that same night.

You see, Grendel stuck again. This time, it was at a restaurant near the inn, so both Sophie and I could respond immediately.

CHAPTER 16

GRENDEL

I had been reading a mystery novel in the living room of our cottage when a prickling sensation broke out all over my body. It was a sign of supernatural activity nearby. I'd had this sensitivity for years, but it was different now.

It was the strong certainty that it was something corrupt and evil—something monstrous. I was pretty sure it was Grendel. He had disturbed my senses like an alarm going off.

This warning was so powerful and unique that it had to be the result of the new powers the Goddess had given me.

I put down my paperback and focused on the sensations. Soon, a vision formed in my head of a restaurant only a block away on the ground floor of a house converted to a bed-and-breakfast. It was a trendy Floribbean eatery whose clientele included the town's movers and shakers.

And the monster, Grendel, crouched in the shadows, behind a hedge near the patio dining area. The Goddess's empathy sensed his every thought and emotion.

He seethed with anger and resentment at the merriment and

jocularity of the crowd. He was jealous. Descended from the corrupted coupling of a fallen angel with a human, the monster was an outcast, loathed by all of mankind. He'd been doomed to suffer in his loneliness and ugliness. He killed and ate people simply as his way of lashing out.

Why was I feeling empathy for him? Because of the Goddess?

But there was no time for empathy. I sensed his anger and stress as he prepared to attack. The rich, spicy scents of the restaurant made his empty stomach growl. His hunger tonight wasn't for human flesh; he also hunted game and probably would have enjoyed one of the blander dishes on the restaurant's menu.

What he truly hungered for was punishment for all those who rejected him.

Sophie! I called out in my mind.

Yes?

Wow, my telepathy was in overdrive. Did I have the Goddess to thank for it?

Grab your sword. We must stop Grendel before he attacks the Carambola Cafe and eats someone important.

It was the kind of crowd that, no matter how panicked they were, would snap photos and videos of the monster attacking them. Hopefully, as a supernatural creature, he wouldn't be captured in the images. But you never know in the world of the eerie.

I was waiting at the main entrance to the inn when Sophie appeared in a T-shirt and cutoff shorts. It wasn't appropriate clothing for the restaurant, but I'm sure they wouldn't mind.

"Did he attack already?" she asked.

"No. He's lurking outside the restaurant, waiting to spring."

"How do you know this?"

"I guess I have extra powers now, courtesy of the Goddess."

We jogged down the cobblestone street, Sophie's sword in its scabbard strapped to her back.

I smelled the garlic and jerk seasoning before I heard the low music and conversation. Grendel hadn't attacked yet. We passed parallel-parked cars and approached pools of light coming from the bed-and-breakfast and the cafe.

"Stay behind me," I whispered. Then I realized I should use my telepathy because Grendel's hearing was probably acute.

I have a gut feeling that my new powers can handle this, though I'm not quite sure how. Don't shoot magic at him unless I ask you to, or if I'm getting my butt kicked.

Okay. She drew her sword.

We crept closer, taking cover on the far side of a car, and then behind bushes and a wrought-iron fence.

Grendel was to our left on the side of the house. I couldn't see him with my eyes, but an image of him formed in my head.

The restaurant was on the right side of the ground floor, its patio taking up half of the historic home's large front porch. Grendel would have to sprint across the front of the house to get to the cafe unless he broke through a window and reached the restaurant via the interior of the house.

A thought came into my mind. He was going to break through the window above where he crouched.

I hummed the Goddess's song. The monster snapped his head to the side and saw me. His nostrils flared above his hideous snout, drinking in the scent of me.

Though he was still hidden from my sight, I saw the hairy, misshapen creature in my mind. Powerfully built with long claws and fangs, covered with shaggy black hair. Eyes that glowed yellow. Though he was humanoid, the human part of him had long ago been transformed into a beast. If he sprang at me, he would be twice my height and four times my weight. All the godlike powers in the world would not keep my human flesh from being torn to shreds.

Grendel, I said to him telepathically while I hummed. *Do not attack these people. We will destroy you in seconds and send you back to Hell.*

He was calculating how long of a leap it would take to reach me.

You do not belong on this earth anymore, I said. *But I can offer you forgiveness for the murders. You can go to a peaceful afterlife. But only after you renounce evil and leave this place.*

Could I do that? As a goddess, was Danu high-ranking enough to send a monster to the Shadowlands as opposed to Hell?

I hummed the song and opened the Goddess's empathy valve even wider.

You will be with your mother in a peaceful place. No more suffering. No more being reviled. Turn away from murder. Give up being a monster. It was not your fault that you were born as a species that humans fear, and they will hate you no longer. Go now. Experience happiness instead of loneliness and shame. I, the Goddess Danu, grant you this.

He gave me the sense that he was taking me seriously.

I know how you feel, I told him. *I know your pain. Leave these people alone, and I will send you somewhere better. If you remain here, you will be destroyed and returned to Hell.*

Why should I believe you? His words came to me in a foreign, bestial tongue, but I understood them.

Because I am the Goddess Danu, the earth mother. I am a healer.

Will you heal me?

Come to me now, and I shall.

A dark shadow detached itself from the house and came toward me. The wrought-iron fence was still between us, but it didn't make me feel much safer.

Sophie tensed behind me and went into a fighting crouch.

"Don't attack him, no matter what," I whispered. "Unless he gets a claw on me."

"Mom, are you sure? This is crazy."

"Let me handle this."

The monster was now right in front of me, with only the bars of the fence protecting me. We were in an unlit part of the property and the backlighting from lights in the bed-and-breakfast and the restaurant made Grendel even darker except for the yellow of his eyes.

His hoarse breath and the beating of my heart were all I heard.

Do you renounce evil? I asked him.

I do not know what evil is. I only do what is in my nature, what humans have forced me to do.

Forget about humans. Think of your soul.

I am part human, he said. *And part angel.*

It doesn't matter. Renounce murder, and I will give you peace.

I sensed confusion in him.

Why did you come back to earth? I asked.

I did not intend to. But my grandfather, the angel, called for me to escape from the Bad Place. I ended up here where there were humans feasting and celebrating. Enjoying pleasures denied me. Making me feel like an outcast again. I wanted to kill them when I was supposed to kill you.

His yellow eyes studied me.

Do you renounce evil? I demanded.

Yes, I do.

I reached through the bars of the fence and put my hand on his arm. Beneath his matted fur was a gnarled hide that felt more crocodilian than mammalian.

"Mom!" Sophie protested.

I ignored her and let the song of the Goddess flow from my lungs. Along with the music, the heat of the Goddess's healing powers flowed from me into Grendel.

The monster trembled and made a mewing cry.

I forgive thee and heal thee, I intoned. *Leave this earth and spend eternity in peace.*

He disappeared.

To be honest, I wasn't sure where he went, whether to Heaven or simply the Shadowlands. I doubted I had the authority to send a soul to Heaven or that he would be allowed in. But the Shadowlands were better than Hell.

And it was better than having him here on earth, eating people.

"That's it?" Sophie asked. "He's gone?"

I nodded.

"That sure was anticlimactic," she said. "I was looking forward to zapping him into dust."

"I never imagined I'd feel empathy for a foul creature like Grendel, but it was what the Goddess wanted. Besides, if his mother has returned to earth, getting rid of him this way is less likely to make her angry. You remember what she did after Beowulf killed Grendel?"

"From now on, are you going to be nothing more than Danu's tool?"

I ignored Sophie's jealous tone and simply shrugged. I didn't know the answer and feared I didn't have a choice.

CHAPTER 17

MOTHER OF A MONSTER

The front door of the cottage burst open. Cory and I sat up in bed, panicked. Our bedroom door was closed, so we couldn't see who had broken in. In my world, I could be pretty sure it wasn't a petty burglar, unless that burglar happened to be supernatural.

There was silence out in the living room. Nothing was moving.

Cory leaped out of bed and found the pistol we kept hidden in the closet. When I grabbed my phone to call 911, I felt the familiar prickling sensation in my hair and extremities that told me our intruder was, indeed, supernatural. So, I called Sophie instead.

"Mom? Is something wrong?"

"Grab your sword and hurry to the cottage," I whispered. "Something just broke in."

Cory moved to the door, gun in hand.

"No," I said. "Don't go out there yet. I don't want the guests to wake up to gunshots. If it's a burglar, let him take our lousy TV and leave."

"I don't want to just sit here while our home is violated."

"You and I both know it's probably not a burglar. And it's probably not human. Let's play it safe."

Something was scratching the bedroom door. It wasn't Cervantes. It was a single digit dragging a nail like it was drawing a picture on the wood.

"Danu, I know you're in there." The voice was feminine, but hoarse and monstrous. "Come out, Danu. I want to see your human face. I want to see who killed my baby."

"It's Grendel's mother," I whispered to Cory. "I was afraid she would come. She escaped through the Veil before we repaired it."

"I didn't kill your son. I sent him gently to the Shadowlands to have the rest he deserved," I said through the door.

"You killed him."

"He died thousands of years ago."

"He was given life again. He was given a second chance. We were all offered the chance to escape and return to earth again."

"You were fooled," I said as sternly as I could, half numb with fear. "The creatures that return to earth through the Veil don't belong here and can never live a real life."

"Because witches and goddesses kill them a second time."

"Let me just shoot this monster," Cory said.

"If she's anything like her son, she'll tear you to pieces no matter how many shots you get off."

I went to the window and opened it.

"What are you doing?" Cory asked, moving to the window to stop me.

"Luring her away from you."

I crawled out the window, landing on a philodendron in a

planter. A light was on in Sophie's room above the courtyard. I hoped she would get here soon.

Cory was at the window I had just left, gesturing for me to come back inside. But I moved across the courtyard, away from the cottage, and hid behind the pump house beside our tiny swimming pool.

I cleared my mind the best I could with a racing heart and drew the Goddess's power into me.

I wished I could fully become the Goddess, but so far, I'd done that only when she wished for me to do so. Also, wouldn't it be dangerous to leave my body standing there frozen while I was battling the monster?

For now, I would gather the Goddess's power like I'd done before and hope my bolts of energy would stop Grendel's mother.

Too late. She stood upright outside of the cottage in the darkness, sniffing for my scent.

In many ways, she resembled Grendel: massive, covered with dark fur, and humanoid. But her head was bony and misshapen, and the horns at her temples were longer and more threatening than her son's. Her jaws were unnaturally large, with lion-like teeth. Her ears were like a wolf's. She had long, human-like fingers with nails that were inches long.

Her head turned and faced in my direction. Her jaws formed the semblance of a smile.

She charged, a loping sprint.

The fire in my stomach raced to my hands, and bolts of white energy shot from my hands and struck her, knocking her backward. She stumbled but remained on her feet.

I sent another blast of lightning at her, hitting her squarely in the chest. The energy crackled all over her body. She wobbled on her feet, then resumed coming at me.

She was almost upon me, and I realized I couldn't stop her.

This was how I was going to die?

Purple lightning struck the monster from the side. The creature dropped onto the cobblestones and writhed in pain.

My daughter crouched in the courtyard, aiming her sword at Grendel's mother. The monster slowly got to her feet, glancing at Sophie and at me, deciding on which of us to attack.

She went for Sophie. And I left the shelter of the pump house and ran after her.

Sophie's next blast stopped the creature in her tracks. I shot my lightning at her. She stumbled.

I ran up to her and pushed her into the swimming pool. She splashed and sank like a stone.

Sophie fired her lightning into the pool, the purple light illuminating the massive dark figure sprawled underwater on the bottom.

"Is the Goddess sending you any empathy?" Sophie asked sarcastically.

"Not at the moment. What took you so long?"

"I got here as fast as I could. It only seemed long to you."

Grendel's mother rose slowly to the surface.

"I guess she's not dead," I said. "Creatures from beyond the Veil disintegrate when they die a second time."

"Are you going to send her off merrily to Heaven or the Shadowlands?" Sophie asked.

I ignored her. Grendel's mother was standing at the deep end. She was so tall, her head and shoulders protruded from the surface. She looked at Sophie and me. Her eyes were yellow and feral.

"Is the Father of Lies your father?" I asked her.

"I know no one by that name." Her voice was gravelly and

stronger than it should have been after all the energy that had struck her.

"Was he a fallen angel?"

The monster grimaced. It was probably a smile.

"He was an angel. More handsome and more intelligent than any man alive. Before he fell, his name was Mendaciel."

"You need to leave," I said. "The Goddess will send you to the Shadowlands, where you can be with Grendel."

"He's not in Hell?" the creature asked, lisping through her fangs.

"No. The Goddess had mercy on him."

"I don't trust you or her."

Grendel's mother waded to the pool's edge and prepared to pull herself out.

Sophie shot more purple lightning at her. It made her stagger backward, and it arced across the surface of the water.

I sent my white lightning at her, as well. The creature staggered further back, then returned to the lip of the pool. She placed her palms on the concrete and pushed herself upward.

Sophie was mouthing words to a spell. I wished she'd spent more time perfecting defensive magic, like immobility or sleep spells. Instead, she preferred to use her power to blow stuff up.

Whatever Sophie was casting didn't work. Grendel's mother was now kneeling on the pool deck.

Sophie screamed like a banshee and swung her sword.

Grendel's mother caught the blade in one hand just before it hit her neck. The palm of her hand was bony cartilage and gripped the blade without injury.

A gunshot rang out, and a clump of fur flew from her torso. She didn't even flinch. Cory fired another round that was just as ineffective.

Suddenly, I felt the Goddess take me over and rise from my

body. I was viewing the scene at the pool from above now, Darla standing there immobile, the monster yanking the sword from Sophie's grasp and tossing it into a palm tree.

"Your magic is weak," she said to Sophie in her gravelly voice. "And you, I'll be back for your daughter," she said to me, but instead of looking at my body down there, she stared up at me hovering above. "You took my son. I shall take *your* child."

She dove back into the pool and swam to the bottom. Then, her body dissipated into a black, ink-like blot and seeped into the drain, disappearing.

I was back in my body, meeting Sophie's surprised eyes.

"Mom, you froze again. Grendel's mother was frightened by that. When she was threatening us, she was looking at the air above you. Did you become the Goddess?"

"I was in the middle of becoming her. Grendel's mother must have sensed it, and it scared her away. We need to find her and destroy her. I don't want to be waiting around for her to come here to kill you."

"I can't argue with that."

"Let me know how I can help," Cory said.

"First, we've got to find her. Sophie and I are going to visit a certain mage who I know is awake at this hour. Maybe he can help us."

ARCH MAGE BOB WAS DETERMINED TO KEEP HIS LIFE AS unchanged as possible, even after being turned into a vampire by Lethia. He worked and surfed at night now, of course. But his surf shop kept its same hours. He barely saw his employees anymore, except when he came in each night a couple of hours before the store closed. None knew he was a vampire, except his closest assistant.

For my purposes, the most important thing that hadn't changed was his magic. While Bob was going through his vampiric transition, his magic had suffered. Today, it is as effective as ever.

"Is this monster physical or not?" he asked in his workshop-office at the back of the store. "Cuz you're like being really vague about it."

"She's not fully of the material world," I answered. "She's physical enough to kill and eat people, but we saw her transform into a liquid state and go down a pool drain."

"So, she's magical?"

"You got it."

"Do you have anything with her energy on it?"

"My sword," Sophie said. "She grabbed onto the blade. Maybe some of her DNA is on it. But no blood. It didn't cut her hand."

Bob frowned and took the sword from her, inspecting it. In his human days, he would have put on a pair of reading glasses. His vampirism obviously improved his vision.

"Yeah." He nodded. "There's a bit of energy on here. Enough to do a locator spell if you guys can chill out for a while. Want anything to drink?"

"I don't want any blood, thank you," I said.

"I was offering a high-sugar, highly caffeinated energy drink."

"Yes, please!" Sophie said.

Bob laid the sword on his workbench and picked up a vial from which he sprinkled powder that looked like sand onto the blade, then leaned over the sword, muttering an incantation. He held his hands, palms up, over the blade, and tilted his head back with his eyes closed.

I felt the magic rush through the room.

Sophie watched her mentor with admiration.

"I see a cave. No, it's an underground room," Bob said, his eyes still closed. "Made of coquina rock. It's really old, probably from the Spanish Colonial days. It's damp in there. Wait, I see why. It's connected to a sewer, a storm sewer, meant to handle seawater when a king tide floods the streets. Old and abandoned."

He was silent for a long time. Sophie and I looked at each other, unsure if it was okay to speak yet.

Bob opened his eyes. "You'll have to drive me around Old Town if you want to locate this room."

So that's what we did. Bob sat in the back seat with the sword in his lap. I drove, and Sophie was in the passenger seat. It was still hours before dawn, and traffic was nonexistent. We rolled slowly along Bayfront Avenue, Bob with his eyes closed again.

When we neared the historic fort, Bob's eyes popped open.

"It's nearby," he said excitedly.

I pulled up outside the closed gate of the visitors' parking lot by the fort's entrance.

"Yeah, it's down there somewhere." He pointed at the fort where its walls met the bay. "Down near the water level. I bet it's in the oldest section of the fort."

"How do we get in there?" Sophie asked. "There are probably alarms and security cameras all over the place."

"We'll go in during the day when the fort is open," I said. "When Grendel's mother is probably asleep. We'll act like tourists and sneak into the parts where we're not supposed to be."

"You'll only be able to access the room from the tunnel," Bob said. "And the tunnel is attached to the sewers. You might be able to get into them just outside of the walls. I'll put an extra enchantment on the sword to last through tomorrow. It will help you locate her."

We thanked him and dropped him off at his shop near the beach. Finally, we headed home to get a couple of hours of sleep.

CHAPTER 18

HARVESTING ENERGY

It seemed like I had just fallen asleep when Cory stirred me awake by getting out of bed. I rolled over to go back to sleep, thinking he was only going to the bathroom, but he pulled clothes on.

"What are you doing?" I mumbled.

"Going to the ley lines with Sophie."

I sat up in bed. "What?"

"She needs extra power to fight Grendel's mother."

"But you swore off magic."

"Like they say, 'desperate times require yada yada.'"

"I'm serious. Getting power from the ley lines takes a tremendous toll on you. You gave that up for your own health."

"Darla, that monster invaded our inn. She could have killed our guests. We must stop her, and Sophie says she needs more energy to do it. Harvesting the ley lines is my special talent. I can't ignore it in a crisis like this."

"The Goddess's power should suffice," I said.

"Really? It scared the monster off our property, but it didn't destroy her. I think the Goddess's power has its limits. You told me it wasn't enough to beat the Father of Lies."

"It wasn't enough at the time. I feel it growing."

"We don't have time to wait for your power to grow. We almost died last night. You said you and Sophie are going to hunt the monster down in her lair. You couldn't kill her in our own home. What makes you think you can kill her in *her* home?"

"Optimism."

He laughed. "You're not an optimistic person. You're optimistic only when you want to rush into something without thinking it through and preparing."

He was right, I had to hand it to him.

"Let me go harvest the ley lines. When I transfer the energy to Sophie, she'll be so much more powerful."

"Okay. But tell me, is this a one-off event, or are you getting back into witchcraft?"

"Maybe I need a hobby to occupy my time when my wife freezes and is off being Danu."

That stung. But I empathized with how he was feeling. One thing about the Goddess, she had a lot of empathy.

I got dressed, too, and we met Sophie at Cory's pickup truck. Sophie and I each had crappy cars, but Cory recently bought an inexpensive truck for carting supplies to the inn. It was one of the few signs I could point to that showed we were finally making a profit.

Cory drove, but I knew I'd be driving on the way home. Harvesting the massive energy from ley lines and transferring it to another witch or wizard left him drained and exhausted. I worried about him sometimes.

A major and minor ley line intersected beneath a park across the street from the waterfront in Old Town, close to the fort. By doing this now, and transferring the energy to Sophie, we were committing ourselves to attacking Grendel's mother this coming day. The power would gradually fade from Sophie if she didn't use it soon.

If the locator spell Bob had used was incorrect, we would lose our window of opportunity. Even worse, depleted of energy, Sophie would be more vulnerable to the monster's attacks.

Cory parked along Bayfront Avenue on the north side of the fort, on the opposite side of where we'd been only a couple of hours ago with Bob. Sophie and I followed him to the park, a tiny triangle of grass dominated by Old Courage, a centuries-old live oak. The giant tree undoubtedly benefitted from the underground energy. We waited on the sidewalk while he strode toward the tree, his expression grim.

I kept glancing around, paranoid that someone was watching us. For all I knew, Grendel's mother was.

He knew this park well, though it had been a while since he last harvested a ley line. That was when he'd been under the influence of an evil wizard who took the harvested power from him like milk from a dairy cow.

Cory reached the tree, then paced off the distance from the trunk. He stood on a spot that looked no different from any other part of the grass, even though it was where the two ley lines intersected. These underground conduits of earth energy connected important holy sites and natural geological points of energy production. Only the weirdest occult followers believed in them.

Until I became one of them.

Cory stood with his back perfectly straight and his arms extended parallel to the ground. After a moment, his body twitched, as if he had been electrocuted.

I caught a faint ozone odor. Then, all my hairs stood on end as the surge of electromagnetic energy left the earth and passed into the body of my husband.

He once told me it was enough energy to kill dozens of people if it had come from a power line. But in this form, absorbed by someone like him with the magic gene, it caused pure euphoria.

Eventually, Cory stepped away from the spot. He staggered, briefly, before heading toward us as if walking on air. I sensed the power radiating from him.

"If you were single, you could probably pick up any woman in San Marcos right now," I said.

He smiled, shaking his head. "The only one who matters right now is your daughter."

Sophie left the sidewalk and met him on the grass, where he knelt before her.

"Put your hands on either side of my head," he said, "and align your inner energy with mine. Then, draw my energy into yourself."

She put a hand over each of his ears and stood silently with her eyes closed.

A loud popping sound was followed by a burst of light that seemed to come from Cory's head. Again, I felt a surge of power.

Sophie's body jerked, and she arched her back. I watched nervously, hoping no one would be hurt.

Finally, she removed her hands and stepped away from Cory. She smiled at me, breathing deeply, her eyes wide and her nostrils flared. Power radiated from her smile.

"Okay," she said. "I'm ready to kick some monster butt."

It was 9:00 a.m., and Sophie and I were the first in line at the fort's ticket booth. We were also the only ones who looked like we hadn't slept in days. The fort complex was a national park, and there was a sign with a list of rules that included the prohibition of weapons.

"Is a sword considered a weapon nowadays?" Sophie asked me in a whisper.

"It's an emotional-support sword."

Sophie carried her sword wrapped in a heavy coat, but at the fort's entrance, a guard stopped her.

"What's wrapped in there?"

"A sword," Sophie said with a huge smile. "I'm a historical re-enactor. I'm going to change into my soldier's uniform inside."

"Oh, of course. Are you going to fire the cannon today?"

"I sure am."

"That was easy," I said as we passed through the thick coquina-stone walls into an interior passageway.

The rest of our visit didn't prove to be as easy.

It had been years since I was last here, so I had to reference the map we were given at the ticket booth. We would avoid the areas where the tourists went: the ramparts atop the walls with colonial Spanish flags and cannons facing the ocean inlet where invading ships once sailed into the bay. We avoided the troop quarters, the hospital, the prison, and all the interesting stuff.

We went in search of stairs to lead us deep into the bowels of the fort. Twice, we continued past signs that said no admittance. When we came to a heavy oaken door that was locked, Sophie used a spell to unlock it. Fortunately, it didn't result in any explosions.

We entered a large, dark room. I turned on my phone's flash-light, which barely penetrated the shadows.

"This should work better," Sophie said, unwrapping her sword from the coat.

She recited an incantation, and the sword glowed with brilliant purple light that illuminated most of the room and its curved stone ceiling. Spanish words painted on the walls revealed that this had once been a facility for storing gunpowder and shot.

At the far end was a wooden trapdoor. A block and tackle hung from the ceiling above. The trapdoor appeared sealed to the stone floor around it from centuries of disuse, and pulling on the metal ring to open it was fruitless.

Again, Sophie used a spell to pull it open with an ear-splitting squeak.

We waited for a few minutes, hoping the noise hadn't caused anyone to investigate. When no one came, I breathed a sigh of relief.

"Your magic is coming in quite handy today," I said.

"I don't think I could have opened that if it weren't for the energy Cory gave me."

A half-rotted wooden ladder led to a dark cavern below. I worried about the ladder's ability to support our descent—or our return, but we had no choice. Sophie descended first, since she had the luminous sword, and I followed.

A cracking sound came from a rung beneath my foot halfway down, and I cringed. Getting back out of here was going to be difficult.

We reached the level below, and the purple light from the sword illuminated a space as expansive as the room above, but with a lower ceiling. The floor was rough-hewn rock that was difficult to walk on without tripping.

"I've lost my sense of direction," Sophie said.

"This way." I pointed toward what I believed was the east. "I can sense the bay nearby. We need to get lower."

I guessed we were close to sea level, beneath the massive earthworks that elevated the fortress above ground level. We carefully walked east until we reached a wall of giant coquina blocks. There was nowhere else to go.

The block and tackle in the gunpowder room suggested that barrels of powder and crates of shot were loaded through the trapdoor we had passed through. That meant there had to be a way to get it in here from the outside. But we couldn't find a door. Maybe there was another trapdoor that we couldn't see.

Faint light to our right caught my eye. We headed in that direction until a narrow opening appeared in the southern wall. We passed through it and the rocky floor sloped downward steeply. Further along the eastern exterior wall of this new space were large metal grates built into the floor. They were the source of the faint light.

We arrived at the nearest grate and looked down. The heavy stone blocks of the fort's exterior sloped down to muddy earth. The ground below looked like it was covered by water during high tides. Just beyond would be the bay, out of our view from this angle.

"Wow!" Sophie exclaimed. "My sword is vibrating. It must be from Bob's locator spell. That means Grendel's mother is nearby."

"I'm guessing the sewers are under the ground down there."

"How can we get to them?"

"We can't get to the land down there from the outside of the fort. Access is blocked off. We could rent kayaks and paddle in from the bay, but it's low tide. We'd have to walk through a long stretch of tidal flats to reach here and probably sink up to our knees in mud. Maybe there's a way to access the sewers farther away from the fort, but who knows where?"

"Or we could take the direct route."

Sophie held her sword in both hands, and its purple glow turned into a blaze. She cut through the ancient metal bars of one corner of the grate like they were butter. They fell to the ground below.

"Sure, go ahead and vandalize a national monument," I said.

Sophie ignored me and climbed through the opening, dropping about eight feet to the ground. I was nervous about making the jump. My daughter gestured impatiently for me to come, and I took the plunge.

At least it was a soft landing. Of course, now there was no way to return the way we'd come. I guess we'd end up wading through mud after all.

That is, if we survived.

CHAPTER 19
SEWER MOUTH

"The sword is telling me she's this way." Sophie turned and headed north along the seawall at the bottom of the fort's towering walls.

The ground rose as we moved northward. Soon, the muddy ground gave way to a ledge of stone blocks. I guessed that this was a wharf of sorts. Did the boats carrying ammunition dock here to load it into the armory above?

Slits in the stone wharf appeared to be for draining water if a wave crested the wharf.

"The sewer tunnel is right below us!" Sophie announced. "And I sense Grendel's mother in there."

"I hope she's sleeping. But how do we get in there? There must be a way for humans to access the tunnel."

"We don't have time to find the way in. And even if we did, what if it was blocked? Grendel's mother can use her magic to slip into the smallest opening, so she would choose a hiding place that no one could get into. I'll use my magic to get in."

Sophie couldn't transform herself into an inky liquid like the monster had. She had to resort to brute-force magic. She hacked at the stone with her glowing sword, but it wasn't working as easily as it had on the metal grate.

The sword's blade was protected from damage by the magic, but it was only dislodging small chunks at a time. Sophie grunted with frustration as she chopped, bathed in sweat.

"Do you still have the energy from the ley lines?" I asked.

Sophie nodded. "But I feel it fading. I'm going to need it to fight Grendel's mother. It's a waste to use it like this, but I have to get in there."

"*We* have to. You're not fighting her alone. I'm going in there, too, with all the power the Goddess will give me."

A large piece of rock broke off and fell into the growing hole Sophie was creating. Since the piece was so large, we heard it land in the space below us. Based on how long it took for the rock to land, the space could very well be a tunnel.

"How foolish you humans are," said a gravelly voice.

Grendel's mother had materialized on the wharf, right beside the hole Sophie was making.

She loomed above us, well taller than Sophie and nearly twice my height. Her yellow eyes and deep growl turned my stomach to ice.

"Sorry to wake you," I said.

Grendel's mother snarled and tried to grab Sophie, who jumped out of her reach just in time.

Sophie swung her sword underhanded, and it clipped the monster's hip. Blood splattered. The power of the ley lines was making the sword deadlier.

I moved to a safe distance and focused on drawing the Goddess's power while I watched Sophie attack Grendel's mother. The monster danced away from each thrust and swing.

Grendel's mother lunged again, and Sophie narrowly eluded

her. I dreaded what would happen if the monster got my daughter in her clutches.

Sophie's sword should have been decisive in this battle, but the monster was too fast at dodging the blade. Clearly, her own magic was making her faster and more agile.

Painful heat was growing in my stomach. My lightning bolts wouldn't be enough to stop the creature, but I hoped they would slow her enough to give Sophie an advantage.

But Sophie stumbled on a chunk of rock she had cut earlier, and the monster grabbed her and held her in a tight bear hug.

"I told you I would get vengeance for my son," Grendel's mother said to me. "Now, I will eat your daughter."

She dissolved into the inky fluid and poured herself into the hole in the rock.

But so did Sophie. The monster's magic turned her into a brown liquid that drained into the sewer below.

Panic and anger surged through me.

And I became the Goddess.

Never get between an earth-mother goddess and her child.

I LEFT MY DARLA-BODY STANDING LIKE A MANNEQUIN ON THE wharf and passed through the hole in the rock.

The sewer tunnel was pitch black, but I, of course, could see. The tunnel was round, made with blocks of coquina smaller than those in the fort's walls. They were covered in barnacles and seaweed and looked like they would eventually collapse. In fact, the tunnel had caved in just behind me and about a hundred feet in front of me. I walked on my bare feet upon rough stones covered with patches of sand and puddles of seawater from the most recent flooding.

My senses filled me with information, but I felt removed from them. For instance, my sense of touch told me when I stepped on a sharp rock, but I felt no pain. The temperature was much lower in here, but I experienced no chills.

You see, my senses did not need to protect a fragile body made of flesh. As a goddess, I didn't have one.

Apart from the scent of saltwater and decaying seaweed, came the smell of the monster. Of wet fur, reptilian skin, blood, and putrescence. And a faint whiff of sulfur from the fires of Hell.

A room of sorts, more of an alcove, was ahead to my left. She was in there with my daughter.

I walked right up to the opening without fear and beheld the monster crouched over Sophie's unconscious body. She looked up at me and snarled.

I hadn't expected her to grab a dagger from the floor and slash me with it. But, of course, I was in pure Goddess form, and the knife had no effect on me. The monster's yellow eyes widened as she realized she could not hurt me.

She tried to dart from the alcove, but I grabbed her neck and forced her to her knees. Her body went limp.

There wasn't a drop of empathy in me like I'd felt for Grendel. His mother was a Nephilim, the offspring of a fallen angel. She was stronger and smarter than her son and even more evil.

Her kind had been removed from earth by God because they were corrupt and wicked. They were like a cancer that needed to be excised for the good of humankind.

I had no empathy, but I would show mercy.

Yet, when I took her hands, with their long nails and palms

like tortoise shells, she began to transform into a fluid once more.

I was faster, though. Before she completed her transformation, I painlessly snuffed out her unnatural life. My power to create life comes with the ability to end it just as easily, and that's what I did to Grendel's mother.

She disappeared from the earth, this time forever.

I took my unconscious daughter in my arms and magically transported her out of the sewer, exiting the hole as easily as I had entered it. Landing in her room at home, I laid her gently on her bed, pouring healing powers into her.

Next, I found myself in a verdant meadow where Cael was waiting for me. I jumped on his bare back and rode until we were among the stars. My destination was the Shadowlands.

My work with Grendel's mother was unfinished.

The Shadowlands were where souls that deserved neither the bliss of Heaven nor the suffering of Hell resided. Many of the inhabitants were humans who hadn't believed in Heaven. But there were also many non-humans, too.

Here, you spent eternity in a setting similar to the land you inhabited when you were alive. I rode along a muddy street of a Scandinavian village from the early Middle Ages. An icy rain fell, though it didn't affect me. Why was it raining? I guess Grendel's mother didn't deserve an afterlife that was too pleasant.

No one was around. The rustic structures looked empty. The only one here was a dark figure running away from me.

I pushed Cael into a gallop and caught up with Grendel's mother. She cowered in fear because she knew why I was here.

I seized her by the hair, and we flew to the gates of Hell.

"I have a new guest for you," I told Hades, pushing the monster into his arms. "By the way, your hound is still running around loose on earth. The city has an ordinance against unleashed dogs. You might want to bring him home."

The Father of Lies will be furious when he discovers I removed his daughter from earth and tossed her into Hell. The good news is that plotting revenge against me will distract him from messing with the Veil.

I WAS DARLA AGAIN, STANDING ALONE ON A STONE WHARF beneath the walls of the fort. I remembered the Goddess had slain Grendel's mother and delivered Sophie to her bed at the inn. How long had I been frozen here?

It occurred to me that I was stranded on this wharf with no way to get out. Thanks, Danu.

There was one way. The tide was coming in, so I took off my shoes and jumped from the wharf into the water. But it was much too shallow for swimming. So, I trudged through the mud flats, past the fort, to a piece of shoreline that allowed me to return to land.

Nearly an hour later, a few people stared at me as I walked through the fort's parking lot covered in mud below my knees. I got into my car feeling good that I could cross a few more items off my supernatural to-do list. Hopefully, someday soon, I could return to normal life running our inn.

Or could I? Would my life ever be normal again?

CHAPTER 20

FALLEN-ANGEL BAIT

On my way home from the fort, Raphael appeared in my back seat. He sniffed.

"Did something die in your car?"

"I thought angels would be impervious to things like unpleasant odors."

"If only that were true."

"By the way, what you're smelling is mud, decayed marine vegetation, sweat, and, well, there might be remnants of a burger in a fast-food bag back there," I said in a tone. "Sorry, but I have a busy life. I've been destroying Grendel, hunting down and destroying his Nephilim mother, then transporting her to Hell. I'm not in the mood for any complaints, okay?"

"My apologies. Humans, as a whole, smell much better today than they did in ancient times, just so you know."

"Why am I lucky enough to have you visit me today?"

"To compliment you on all your great work."

"Knock off the nonsense." I wasn't taking anything from anyone, not even a gorgeous, archangel.

"I'm here about The Watchers. We've been monitoring the situation, and we believe the Father of Lies and Lucifer have recruited enough newly fallen angels to be Watchers and to establish a colony on earth. All they need is human wives. And humans are quite easy for angels to seduce."

"Don't be so full of yourself."

"I'm referring to fallen angels, of course, who are morally lacking."

"What does this have to do with me? I don't know any gullible women."

"We need your help in finding out where The Watchers will live."

"But why me? Danu is not the goddess of naughty hook-ups."

"We've been surveilling the fallen angels. And one of them, Armaros, has been visiting your daughter."

"She told me about that. I put a stop to it. I believe he came to our inn because so many angels do to serve as gateways, or on visits such as yours."

"And he probably sensed her magical powers. We need you to tell her to lead him on, feigning interest, so we can find out where he takes her."

"Do you think it would be where the original Watchers lived on earth?"

"It could be anywhere." He reached down under the front passenger seat and held up a paper fast-food bag. "I found your decomposing hamburger."

Then, he disappeared.

"YOU WANT ME TO BE FALLEN-ANGEL BAIT?" SOPHIE ASKED incredulously.

"That's what Raphael wants."

"You told me how horrible The Watchers are and how dangerous it would be for me to date one."

"I know. I'm sorry. You need to lead him on without letting anything happen. As soon as you find out where The Watchers are going, you can escape his clutches. I'll help you. So will the angels."

"I don't know. What if he doesn't visit me again? I don't know how to get in touch with him."

"He's attracted to you and your magic. He'll be back."

"How can you be so sure? He's an angel. He's not a typical man."

"He's a fallen angel. They're more depraved than a bunch of guys at a bachelor party."

"Aren't you worried about me?"

"I am, but any angel who thinks he can control you will have another thing coming."

To be honest, I *was* worried about using Sophie to gather intelligence on The Watchers. However, that she successfully broke up with the Fae God of War made me confident that she wasn't a pushover to deities and the like.

The worst part was waiting for Armaros to contact Sophie again. She didn't have the angel-summoning power I had, so she used magic to call for him. Meanwhile, I was bracing for an attack from the Father of Lies in revenge for destroying Grendel and his mother.

As I came into my goddess powers, I discovered I had a much greater ability for sensing the presence of the supernatural. In the past, I would get all prickly when a ghost, demon, or monster was nearby. Now, I could sense gods and angels, as well.

So, when my divine radar alerted me that an angel had entered the inn, and it wasn't visiting me, I raced upstairs. Yep, I was eavesdropping outside of Sophie's room like an overly protective mother.

The walls and doors of our inn are thick enough to cut off most noise and allow a good night's sleep. So, I couldn't hear what they were saying, only the low murmur of voices. And my telepathy was blocked by Armaros's presence in the room.

After a while, they got louder and more animated. I heard Sophie shouting.

I banged on the door. "Everything okay in there?"

Sophie opened the door and stuck her face out.

"We were having a discussion," she said.

I got a glimpse of Armaros standing by her bed. His wings were out and unfolded. I supposed it was to impress Sophie, but they were black, like a crow's wings. I'd only seen Raphael's wings once since he usually hid them beneath his celestial garb.

Raphael's wings were pure, snowy white, like you'd expect with an angel. Not black like these.

Armaros's aura was visible. It was black, too. This angel was obviously fallen with no way to hide it.

"Are you in fear for your safety?" I asked Sophie.

"There is no need to be concerned," Armaros said. "I shall leave now. Sophie, until tomorrow, my dear."

The surrounding air shimmered, and he disappeared.

"Was he fresh with you?"

"Yeah, he was. He wanted to get intimate and couldn't believe that I refused. Especially after I agreed to travel with him to the Promised Land."

"Ah, so The Watchers *are* settling in Israel like they did before."

"No, the Promised Land is the name of an all-inclusive resort in the Bahamas. It's one of those cheesy ones for singles and swingers. Ugh."

"I don't understand. Why would he take you on a vacation?"

"The resort is where The Watchers are going to live. They'll meet human women there and raise their little Nephilim, turning the place into a compound where they're worshiped like false gods."

"Like cult leaders," I added.

"Cult leaders who never die."

I shuddered at the thought. Would their Nephilim turn out as monstrous as Grendel's mother?

"Thank you for getting this information," I said. "You've done all we needed from you."

"But I have to go to the Promised Land."

"Absolutely not! Why in the world would you want to do that?"

"Armaros is picking me up tomorrow. If I refuse to go, he'll be suspicious. Or worse, he might abduct me. If I go with him, I can escape right before the angels attack The Watchers."

"I don't know what the angels' attack plans are and when they'll execute them. Every minute you're there, you'll be in danger from Armaros's lust."

Sophie considered this. "Yeah, you're right. I'll need to stay in hiding tomorrow and have a guardian angel look out for me."

As soon as I returned to the cottage, I called for Raphael. He arrived almost immediately, and I reported what Sophie had told me.

"The Bahamas?" Raphael was mystified. "I guess the world is so much smaller now than it was back in the beginning of human history."

"May I ask you a personal question? Your wings are always white, correct?"

He laughed. "Yes. Do you want to see them?"

"That's not necessary. Armaros's wings are black."

"Yes, fallen angels' appearances reflect their corruption and evil natures. Eventually, their beauty fades and they become loathsome. Just like their children. The human women who mate with fallen angels are in for a rude surprise a few years from now."

"Please protect Sophie from that fate."

"Of course."

But it was already too late. My telepathy picked up the beginning of Sophie's scream before it was blocked.

Raphael disappeared as he rushed inside to intervene.

"Cory!" I shouted. "Sophie's been abducted."

He ran out of our bedroom, in boxers and a T-shirt, and into the inn.

It was time for me to be the Goddess. When a loved one was in danger, my transformation was instantaneous.

I left my body behind and soared into the sky, to the upper reaches of our atmosphere, searching for my baby.

She was already in the sprawling cluster of islands not far from the Florida peninsula. The Bahamas.

I dove to the earth again, zeroing in on a minor island of the chain, more of a cay. I planned to swoop right in, scoop up my baby, and bring her home.

But I hit resistance. A force of energy protected the part of the island where the resort was and where the fallen angels had gathered. They were trying to protect themselves from God's angels. And it worked against me, too.

I've been slowly learning my powers, as well as their limits. So far, I hadn't been able to defeat the Father of Lies, a senior fallen angel. I believed I should be able to wipe out the newer ones, but when they congregated and amassed their collective force, I simply couldn't break through their shield.

I returned to my body in our cottage. Cory returned, cursing under his breath about the abduction of Sophie. This was how I comforted him:

"Let's do a getaway to the Bahamas."

"Are you crazy? Sophie's been taken."

"A resort called the Promised Land is where she is. Good thing The Watchers haven't completely taken over the resort yet."

"Isn't that one of those sleazy singles' places?"

"Yes. And Danu can't break through the protective shield the fallen angels have. But maybe Darla can enter as a human."

"What about the inn?"

"Bella can run it. We'll be gone for a very short time."

"How do you know?"

"Because I will attack as soon as I can. We're not there to eat at buffets and sit around in hot tubs."

"I would never hang out in a hot tub in a place like that."

"That makes two of us. I'll buy tickets now. Are you in?"

"I will not sit here while you and Sophie fight for your lives. Besides, I could never handle breakfast and Teatime without one of you helping me."

"Okay. Pack your skimpiest bathing suits. Next stop: the Promised Land."

CHAPTER 21
ANGEL ACTION

"I'll have another Bahama Mama," Cory said to the bartender near the swimming pool.

A steel-drum band played Calypso tunes while women and men, mostly young, swam and sunbathed by the pool or played volleyball on the beach.

"We're here to rescue Sophie, not to enjoy ourselves," I said to Cory.

Of course, we were wearing bathing suits—to fit in among the crowd—and sitting at the outdoor bar. We were supposed to be mistaken for ordinary resort guests.

"We haven't had a vacation in years," Cory said. "Even goddesses need to chill out sometimes."

"I can't relax when Sophie is held captive."

"I know. But you need to act like you're relaxing so we don't attract attention."

"We're too old to fit in with this crowd," I said, nodding toward the youthful bodies on display. I had seen a flamboyant older married couple who were probably swingers, and a couple of creepy older men leering at the young flesh in bikinis, but the guests were largely in their twenties and thirties.

Women who were at their peak of fertility. Exactly what The Watchers were craving. But I didn't see The Watchers at the pool or beach, unless they were taking on personas that didn't look angelic.

"I've wandered every inch of this resort and seen no sign of Sophie," Cory said. "I'm guessing she's in one of those cottages down the beach from here."

"I agree. There's a strong psychic barrier around that entire section of the resort. I can't approach it, even as Darla, because Danu is in me."

"And you don't want them to know Danu is here." He glanced at his watch. "Let me walk over there and see if the housekeepers are in any of the cottages. If they leave a door open while they're working, I'll peek inside."

As he walked away in his T-shirt, bathing suit, sandals, and shades, I could tell he was making a determined attempt not to gawk at the women in the hot tubs he passed.

I knew the angels were within striking distance of the resort: Raphael, Gabriel, Michael, Uriel, and several others. Raphael wouldn't tell me what their plans were. He only promised that Sophie would be rescued.

I worried, though. She could be hurt if there was a battle, or Armaros could escape and take her with him, fleeing to who knows where. I wanted to free her as soon as possible.

"Can I buy you another drink?" asked a young man sidling up to the bar beside me. He had blond hair and the bland, mildly handsome face you'd find in abundance at prep schools. He was shirtless and seemed eager to show off his defined six-pack abs.

"Thank you, but I'm good."

"Whatcha drinking? Vodka?" He slurred his words, and it wasn't yet noon.

"Club soda."

"Oh." He sounded disappointed. He took a gulp of his beer. "Have you been here before? This is my first time. I'm with a bunch of buddies."

"It's our first time, too. My husband and I."

He raised his sunglasses and squinted at me with disappointment.

"There's lots of hot chicks here, but I like more mature women."

I didn't answer.

"You know, the ones they call cougars."

"Not many of those here."

"I was kind of hoping you were one."

The fact that he was drunk made me forgive him. To a point.

"I told you I was married. My husband will be right back."

My tone offended him. "Yeah, well, you're kinda old for a cougar, anyway."

I'm sorry, I couldn't help myself. Or Danu couldn't help herself. I pointed my index finger at his forehead and a quick burst of lightning hit him, snapping his head backward. His flailing hand knocked over his beer as he stumbled away from the bar, careening off a pool butler, and landing in a hot tub with the older swinger couple.

"Cut that guy off," I said to the bartender.

My victim seemed to be recovering from the minor dose of goddess power. He was making fast friends with the swingers in the tub.

Cory returned. "Man, there's beer spilled all over my barstool."

"Did you see anything at the cottages?"

"No. That shield doesn't seem to affect a mere human like me, but I couldn't get close to them because there's a guard patrolling the area."

"A security guard from the resort?"

"He wasn't in a uniform. The guy was a real freak. Had to be seven feet tall, minimum, and was super muscular. Hairy, too. I'm not even sure he was human."

"He sounds like a Nephilim." I had previously educated Cory on the children of The Watchers and human women. "The Watchers must be more established on earth than the angels realized. I'll send word to Raphael."

The angel visited our hotel room that afternoon. It was the first time Cory had met him, and they were cordial toward each other. I tried hard to hide any sign of swooning over the gorgeous archangel.

"Yes, we are aware of the Nephilim," Raphael said aloud, so that Cory could hear him, too. "The new Watchers have sired young Nephilim in various parts of the world, and when they establish their community here, all of them will come."

"That won't help the Bahamian tourism industry," Cory said.

"No."

"At this resort, do The Watchers only seduce single women?" I asked.

"They take whomever they want. If the women have boyfriends or husbands, the men will be mesmerized into leaving the resort. Or they will be killed."

I glanced at Cory. He should feel relieved that I was allegedly too old to be a cougar.

"When are you going to attack?" I asked Raphael.

"I cannot say. We will determine when the time is right. We want as many Watchers here as possible when we do so."

"Does that include the Father of Lies?"

Raphael didn't answer. He only smiled.

"We can't wait," I said. "We must rescue Sophie before she's overcome by Armaros. I can't get into the area where The Watchers are staying because they put up a barrier shield to keep the Goddess out. Can you help us, Raphael?"

"We can't let The Watchers know we're here before we attack. I have faith you will prevail," he said as he faded away.

I was frustrated. Yeah, angels are amazing and ridiculously attractive, but they had their own agenda. Humans were rarely their priority.

I asked Cory what he thought of Raphael, and how he would describe the angel's beauty.

"It's funny," he replied. "Raphael looks just like the angels in medieval and early Renaissance art. A little feminine, a little awkward."

Yeah, the angels appear to humans in whatever form the humans had in their minds. Cory went for the retro look. My imagination had a more idealized image.

THAT EVENING, CORY AND I SPENT ALL OUR TIME IN THE public areas of the resort, hoping to spot The Watchers. After a bland meal, we hung out at the pool bar until the people in the hot tubs got too frisky. We moved inside, where the main lounge had a DJ.

Just as I was considering calling it a night, The Watchers wandered in. Thirteen good-looking men, around the same age as the main demographic of the resort, sat at neighboring tables in the back of the room. Dressed as normal, stylish humans, they had no outward signs of being angels, let alone fallen ones. I immediately sensed that they were, of course.

One thing you couldn't deny, The Watchers exuded charisma. It was supernaturally based, but that didn't stop women from passing by their tables. The Watchers spoke to them, which we couldn't hear over the music, and the women inevitably sat down.

If a woman had come to the lounge with a boyfriend or husband, the jilted man would mysteriously leave the place without a word. Supernaturally induced, of course.

What mattered most to me was that Armaros was not among them. I pointed it out to Cory.

"He must be in his cottage with Sophie," I said. "I'm going there. Maybe the protection shield there is weaker since the others are in here."

Cory touched my arm to urge caution, but I was already getting up and rushing out of there. I hurried down the sandy path that led to the cluster of cottages. Occasional landscape lights lit the path, and it wasn't until I was in view of the cottages, with their dim front-porch lights, that I felt the protective magic.

As I had hoped, it was much weaker now. If I became Danu, her power could break through. Because of my concerns as a mother, I became the Goddess instantly and left Darla standing there behind a palm tree while I searched for the right cottage.

There, on the right—the tiny pastel-blue clapboard house was where Sophie and Armaros were.

In my goddess form, I passed quietly through the crack beneath the door to find Sophie huddled in a corner beside the sofa in the living room. Armaros stood above her, black wings outstretched.

"Your magic has only slowed me," he said to her. "It can't stop me. Submit to me willingly. You will be happy you did."

"I don't think so," I, Danu, said.

I slammed into the angel and threw him across the room into the wall. When he slid to the floor, landing on his butt, he turned to me, wild-eyed. His hands made a complex gesture as he attempted to use demonic magic against me.

But he was a newly fallen angel, pathetically weak compared to me.

"Get out of here," I said. "You don't belong on earth, nor in Heaven."

"You don't tell me, an angel, what to—"

I smacked him in the head, grabbed him by the wings, and tore off their feathers. Then I picked him up and carried him on my shoulder.

By the way, Darla was petite. Danu could be whatever size she wanted.

I threw the stunned fallen angel across the back of my horse, who had appeared beside me. Then, I rode with my captive to the stars, through the Veil, and to the gates of Hell.

"Enjoy your stay in this resort," I said as I dumped him into the abyss.

When I returned to the cottage on earth, I unlocked the door. Then I returned to Darla, still standing frozen on the path.

When I woke up again in my human form, I went inside the cottage, where Sophie engulfed me in an embrace.

"The Goddess—you—saved me," she said, weeping.

"You risked everything to help us find The Watchers. You're the hero here."

I brought Sophie to our room and went to the lounge to retrieve Cory. He had been hitting the Bahama Mamas and wanted to dance, but I told him we were taking the first flight out in the morning.

When we left the lounge, each Watcher had a woman sitting next to him or in his lap.

Truth was, Cory and Sophie weren't flying out in the morning. I became Danu again and transported them to San Marcos before returning to the island to fetch my physical self. I tried to summon a gateway to bring me—Darla—home.

But no angel would respond. Later that night, I discovered why.

A terrible thunderstorm swept in. At least, that's how it would appear to the humans on the island. In reality, it was an attack by the angels on The Watchers. Because of my supernatural sensitivities, I saw exactly what was going on.

It was like an air raid: angels swooping in to blast the compound with lightning. Explosions sounded like thunder. Raphael and the other archangels flew close to the ground, their giant white wings beating, casting the giant lightning bolts like spears into the collapsing cottages. I alone could see the angels; any human witnesses would only see the lightning.

The Watchers cowered in their cottages, except for a few who rushed outside to face their attackers. Their demonic fireballs fell harmlessly to the ground after missing the angels. The Watchers' demonic magic stirred up a tornado that threatened to suck the angels to earth, but instead, it destroyed their own cottages.

I don't know what happened to the human women who went home with them, but The Watchers were quickly defeated.

They had all been junior angels, so even if they hadn't fallen, they would never be a match for Raphael, Michael, Uriel, and the other archangels. And after The Watchers had fallen from grace, they lost their angelic powers. They had demonic powers now, but they were much weaker than those of the Father of Lies.

Raphael had hoped the Father of Lies would be here, so the group of angels could finish him off. But he was missing.

Once the battle was over, the angels carried The Watchers to Hell and tossed them in a lake of fire and brimstone, where they were condemned to remain for eternity.

After it was over, the drunken preppie who was looking for a cougar wandered by where I was standing watching the battle.

"Too bad the fireworks show was ruined by the thunderstorm," he said to me.

"You got that right."

"Want to hang out in the hot tub?"

He must have forgotten what I'd done to him earlier. When I pointed at his forehead, he suddenly remembered. He walked away quickly for a drunk guy. Until he collided with a palm tree with a loud *bonk* of his head on the trunk.

Again, I asked for an angel to give me a ride home.

And that was when the Father of Lies showed up.

CHAPTER 22

YOU CAN'T HANDLE THE TRUTH

The demon's power hit me like a rogue ocean wave, throwing me into the drywall of our hotel room and knocking the wind out of me. The door flew open, and a magnificently handsome man walked inside toward me.

I had pepper spray in my purse. I was pretty sure it was useless against him.

He had jet-black hair and flint-gray eyes. His prominent chin had a dimple. His clothing was blindingly white.

I'd never seen him before, but I knew who he was.

"This is how you looked before you fell?" I asked the Father of Lies.

He nodded. "My name was Mendaciel, and I was among God's inner circle of angels. I was as naïve then as Raphael and the others are now."

I nodded, killing time until I could become the Goddess again. I didn't stand a chance against him unless I was fully Danu. And even then, my power might not be enough to prevail.

"The world had already been created. God's masterpiece was

complete. All that was needed was to maintain and nurture His creation, help new species evolve, and watch as jungles turned to deserts and rivers carved canyons. All we did was bicker among ourselves as to which angel was most favored."

"Not your kind of thing?"

"When God created humans, I saw a tremendous opportunity. Lucifer took away their innocence, and then they were allowed to spread across the planet like animals, albeit smarter, more dangerous ones. While I taught them how to deceive and manipulate others, I was doing the same to them."

"Hence your name, the Father of Lies."

He ignored me. "As I watched the humans blunder their way into civilizations, I took a liking to human women. There was a group of us who wanted the delights of human flesh. Our silver tongues could convince any women we wanted. And we made a pact among us, The Watchers, to be our own gods among humans."

He towered over me. Why wasn't I Danu yet? My fight against Armaros must have exhausted me.

"The angels destroyed what we were building and banished us from earth. They made me look like this."

The handsome angel was no longer there. Now, the decaying old man, who'd been revealed to me in my bedroom nearly a year ago, stood before me.

"However, I escaped and returned to earth, manipulating humans again. As you creatures learned new methods of communication, my job became easier. Spreading lies and conspiracy theories allowed me to warp your societies. I can create civil wars and world wars. I could make your species wipe itself out with my lies and persuasion if I wanted to. That is true God-like power."

I nodded. Danu, where are you?

"Now you and those silly angels are meddling once again as I try to reestablish The Watchers. All I want is to immerse myself in human women and forget about that treacherous vampire, Lethia. Why are you, a forgotten pagan goddess, getting in my way?"

"Because you made an enemy out of me. You helped the Fae tear the Veil and send monsters to kill me and to harm this earth that is my child. The earth is good, and you are evil. And you must be driven away."

"You speak of your child. You destroyed *my* child and her son."

"Your Nephilim didn't belong on the earth. If you cared for her and her son, you wouldn't have brought them here."

Mendaciel, the Father of Lies, surprised me as emotion overcame him.

"My daughter rejected me," he said. "She left our community and wandered far away into the frigid north."

As much as it was in my nature, I couldn't feel empathy for him. My anger and defiance grew until I suddenly became Danu and saw the demon's true appearance. As I, Danu, stood behind the decaying bag of bones that was the Father of Lies, Darla sat on the floor in front of him, her eyes glazed over.

I tapped the demon on the shoulder. "Old man, I'm back here."

He turned and smiled lasciviously. "Such a pretty goddess."

I punched him, knocking the decaying flesh from his skull. I know, I know, punching isn't the kind of thing deities do. It just felt so good.

We were no longer in the hotel room, but in a space somewhere between earth and sky. We fought like two falcons, crashing into each other, biting, and clawing, before breaking free to circle around again. And come at each other once more.

I was more powerful now than the last time we'd battled. As I came into my identity as Danu, I could access more of her power. She was not a goddess of war. She was a healer. But, like nature, she could destroy and excise the harmful. Like the Father of Lies.

Not she, I. I am Danu.

The demon was a disease harming the health of humankind, who, in turn, was harming the planet and its creatures. He must be excised.

The only antidote to lies was truth. And truth was entwined with knowledge. While the Father of Lies and I fought each other like birds of prey, I forged a mental connection with the members of the Memory Guild. I connected with each of them individually, and collectively as the team we had formed, working together to preserve knowledge and the truth.

I reached out to Dr. Noordlun, to Archibald, and to Diego. I connected with my fellow psychometrist, Laurel. I touched the minds of Summer, James, Diana, Gloria, and Sage.

And together, we connected with the Tugara, who contained the archives of all the memories we preserved.

I felt more confident having the rock-solid nature of truth and knowledge with me, as well as the spirit and dedication of the Guild members. They were my friends and family. And from them I drew power, as well.

The same with my own human family. The Father of Lies was nothing but a demon. Whereas I, Danu, was the mother of the earth. And, as Darla, I was a mother and a daughter and a wife. A valued member of my community.

I drew power from these relationships, as well.

Finally, I realized that the power the Father of Lies had over me was itself a lie, an illusion. His power came from destruction and negation, from death and nothingness.

My power came from birth and regeneration. From health and fecundity. From life that grew and spread, and filled the world with oxygen, and made it green with forests and blue with seas teeming with life. My power came from the rich soil, all its nutrients, and all the microorganisms within it.

The only things the Father of Lies had were hatred and lies.

I had love and truth. And the irrepressible urge for living things to survive, grow, and reproduce.

I was on the side of being. He was about nothingness.

And ever since the universe was created, my side was the winning side.

Seizing the demon's shoulders as we soared in the realm between worlds, I stared into the empty sockets that were his eyes. And everything I was feeling and knowing—and all the truths the Memory Guild had collected—poured from me into him.

It was too much for him to bear. He had no defense against the truth and the power of life.

He screamed a soulless wail as he dissolved, and my hands were left touching nothing.

He was gone.

Who knows where he went and in what form? I assumed he was in Hell, and perhaps he could return. But for now, he was no longer a threat to anyone.

When I returned to my body in the hotel room, Raphael was sitting in the reading chair. Well, I doubted that anyone at a resort like this read books. Let's call it the TV-watching chair.

"We saw what you did," he said, smiling, a ray of sunshine literally coming from his white teeth, "and we applaud you."

"You let me fight him alone?"

"He was supposed to be in the cottage compound when we attacked, but the wily old demon escaped just before. By the time we discovered he was in here, you already had the situation well in hand."

"I don't know why you didn't take care of him years ago while he was messing with humans."

"Other than the guardian angels, most of us don't get involved in human affairs unless it's of global importance."

"I would think a demon using lies and conspiracy theories to turn people crazy and kill each other would be of global importance."

He shrugged. "Humans are mentally frail."

"Yes, which makes me wonder why you first started visiting this frail-minded human, even if I was a vessel for the Goddess."

"You're the perfect vessel. As she very well knows."

"I still don't understand why an angel like yourself, a divine entity in Christianity, Judaism, and Islam, is working with a forgotten pagan goddess."

He smiled again, almost blinding me. "Each religion is a product of a culture's attempt to understand where the world came from and how to find meaning in life. We're all the children of the Creator, regardless of what name or names you give him or her. The Goddess was trying to return to earth because the earth needs her now more than ever."

"But where does she fit in with you angels?"

"I consider her to be a very powerful angel. We couldn't have healed the Veil, but she could. So, we'll simply have to work together."

"What is she—I guess I should say, what am I—supposed to do now?"

"You will learn your next task when it presents itself."

"What if I don't want any more tasks?"

"Oh, but you will. You are the Goddess. You'll be able to continue your human life as is, but when the Goddess is needed, you will want to answer the call."

I didn't like that answer, but I had to admit I appreciated the power to save my family. I just had to make sure they stopped getting into situations where they needed saving.

"I have another question," I said. "Why do angels serve as gateways for me and others? I first went through one long before the Goddess was in me."

"We knew the Goddess was in you long before you did. As I've said before, one job of the angels is to transport recently departed souls to Heaven, to Hell, or for those whose fate is uncertain, to the In Between. We also have helped people who are alive travel to and from the In Between to escape persecution."

"But you took my husband from me years ago when he accidentally went through a gateway disguised as a closet door. And I have a gateway frequently showing up in the inn disguised as an attic."

Raphael looked like he was losing patience with me.

"Sometimes, we have motives beyond human comprehension," he said. "Other times, mistakes may have occurred."

I laughed. "You sound like a corporate executive. 'Mistakes may have occurred.'"

"As I've said, the most junior angels serve as gateways. Some have specific territories. A wizard once lived at your inn, and he was frequently taken to the In Between for his own safety. These angels linger in the same places out of habit."

"Sort of like taxis and ride shares hanging out where they know they'll get fares?"

"There is much more to the supernatural world than you have experienced. There is much more to your city than you know."

"Tell me more."

"Your Memory Guild hasn't found all the memories of your city. There are secrets buried there from when the Spanish first colonized it, and from before Europeans arrived. Long before."

"Really?"

"Why do you think so many legendary monsters went there, even after they were no longer directed to kill you? They appeared in other cities, but most came to yours. Why?"

"I'm waiting for you to tell me."

"The answers are buried deep beneath the city. You will learn them when you need to."

On that note, he disappeared.

I was furious that he wouldn't tell me what the secrets were, but not surprised. Angels seem to delight in being mysterious. Perhaps Dr. Noordlun has the answers.

Eager to leave the so-called Promised Land, I tried to summon a gateway. "Tried" being the operative word because no angel responded.

"Wait, don't I get a ride out of here?"

I kept trying, but no gateway arrived to take me home. I guess my hard questions about them didn't help.

I called the airline to change my reservation to the earliest flight to Florida tomorrow. It was a horrible price, in a horrible seat, but even a goddess must sit in the middle seat sometimes.

CHAPTER 23

DOGCATCHER

I called Dr. Noordlun after I returned home. When I first joined the Memory Guild, protocol held that I couldn't contact him directly; I had to go through an intermediary, such as Archibald.

Now, I had his personal number. All my work with the Guild had bought me some respect. That and being a goddess, I guess.

"I heard a rumor that there are secrets buried beneath San Marcos," I said. "Any truth to that?"

"Well, of course, any city as old as ours has artifacts and historical clues buried beneath it. Whenever there's an archeological dig here, the deeper you go, you uncover older and older layers."

"An angel told me this. I don't think he was referring to Colonial Spanish pottery shards."

Dr. Noordlun was silent for a while. I wondered if he'd hung up.

"As chair of the college's history department, I've heard rumors," he said. "Mostly crackpot theories. Everything from

Vikings visiting here long before the Spanish to an extinct intelligent species. Space aliens, even." He chuckled. "You needn't concern yourself. The Memory Guild is always vigilant about finding clues about things like this."

I thanked him and said goodbye, not satisfied.

Mom invited Cory, Sophie, and me to dinner that evening. Her favorite local seafood market had received a large catch of blue crabs, so Mom steamed a few dozen in seasoned water and set out a feast on the picnic table in her backyard. The table was covered with newspapers, and there were plenty of paper towels on hand for the messy work of cracking open the crabs to get to their sweet meat. The main dish was accompanied by corn-on-the-cob, coleslaw, potatoes, baked beans, and ice-cold beer.

The evening was warm, but not too humid, and the rosy glow of the setting sun gave us enough light to eat, assisted by two lanterns on the table. The backyard was fenced off from the neighbors and had a giant live oak with a tire swing from my childhood still hanging from one of its great limbs.

My family of witches couldn't resist using their magic to levitate the food bowls and platters, passing them around in the air. Here I was, a goddess, but I didn't have the ability to do that. Not that I needed to, but I felt left out. I supposed Danu could transport the food to another planet, or something like that, but little party tricks were not in her skill set.

Interestingly, my family's magic didn't include any spells to make picking out the crabmeat any easier. They still had to get vinegar, melted butter, and seasonings all over their fingers as they harvested the meat revealed by their wooden mallets and nutcrackers.

"How was your trip to the Bahamas?" Mom asked.

"It was lovely," I said. "Just a little getaway to bring the family together."

Cory snorted. "It was a sleazy singles resort."

"Why would you choose to go there? What was it called again?"

"The Promised Land," I replied. "Someone recommended it."

"Oh, isn't that the place that had a tornado and a big fire? I heard about it on the weekend news."

Mom was aware of most of the supernatural stuff going on in San Marcos, but she didn't need to know about everything I experienced. I figured at her age, too many revelations could be unsettling.

Speaking of unsettling. . .

The hoarse barking of a pack of dogs came from the front yard. The barks sounded too familiar to ignore.

Sure enough, trotting along the side of the house came three-headed Cerberus.

"Dang! I left my sword in the car," Sophie said.

"My goodness!" Mom exclaimed.

"It's the hound who guards the gates of Hell. He slipped through the Veil before it was repaired," I explained. This was exactly the kind of revelation Mom did not need.

The three heads had been sniffing the ground, but as the monster dog entered the backyard, he caught our scents.

And growled at us.

"Can you cast your immobility spell without your sword?" I asked Sophie.

"No. Sorry."

Cerberus trotted toward us.

"I think we're all going to be sorry. Don't worry, Mom. We'll defend you."

Mom was frozen with fear, a crab claw in one hand and a mallet in the other. Neither was going to save her. Mom had been less frightened than this when a hostile vampire had been in her kitchen, but she didn't like large dogs. And Cerberus was beyond large.

"I learned an immobility spell from Texas Tom," Cory said. He got up from the table to put himself between us and the hellhound.

Before he could utter a word of the spell, Cerberus had the seat of Cory's pants in one of his mouths and was shaking him like a rope toy.

No time for me to gather the power to shoot white lightning. Seeing my husband about to be devoured turned me into the Goddess.

I left Darla behind and strode confidently to the hellhound. I raised my arm in command.

"Stop!" I shouted in an ancient language Danu knew, but I didn't. "Release him!"

Cerberus's three heads whimpered. The one that held Cory dropped him, and Cory crawled away on the grass, then walked slowly back to the table.

"Lie down!"

The giant beast obeyed.

The chain that served as a collar at the base of the three necks was still intact. I grabbed it.

"Come," I commanded.

I tugged on the collar and led Cerberus to my horse, who had just appeared near the fence. Cael wore a loose coil of rope around his neck. I removed it and tied one end to the dog collar and wrapped the other end around my hand. Mounting my horse, I gave the rope a gentle but brisk yank.

"Come," I said to the hellhound as I rode the horse through the side yard.

And suddenly, we were soaring past the stars. The Veil parted to allow our passage through it.

We descended to the gates of Hell. Not surprisingly, there was no doorbell.

"Hey, Hades!" I called. "I've got your pooch."

Hades emerged from the darkness and walked up to the other side of the gate. Not to be confused with Lucifer or Satan, Hades was merely the landlord of this infernal place. The dark-bearded god, brother of Zeus, wore a helmet and carried a large key.

"Cerberus! Where have you been?" he asked as he unlocked the gate. "Thank you so much for returning him. Would you like a reward?"

"Uh, no thanks. I know how it hurts to lose a pet, and frankly, I wanted him out of my city."

I handed Hades the rope, and he led his hellhound through the gate.

"That's my boy," he said in a baby-talk voice, crouching in front of Cerberus and giving each head an affectionate rub. "No more running away. You be a good boy and stay here with Daddy."

All three heads barked in joy. I waved goodbye and got back on my horse.

When I returned to earth and became Darla again, I found Mom staring at me with a concerned expression.

"You scared me!" she said. "Sophie said you've been freezing like this a lot lately."

"Yes, when I fully become the Goddess. I go off and do, well, goddess stuff. And leave my human body behind for just a little while. C'mon, I was frozen for less than a minute, right?"

"It seemed like hours," Mom replied. "I thought it was a seizure."

"Not at all."

"You should see a doctor and have this looked into. Get an MRI or something like that."

"Mom, don't worry. I've fully evolved into my role as Danu. The good news is I can still be Darla, too. The only downside is I freeze for a few seconds."

"It seemed like forever. I think you're taking this goddess thing too far, dear."

"You were okay with it when I first told you. You joked about it."

"I fully support you with your psychometry, the Memory Guild, and all that. I support Sophie's education as a witch, and even Cory's . . . whatever he thinks he's doing. But, really, a goddess?"

"Yes. A goddess. Didn't you see me, as Danu, capture the three-headed dog?"

"No. The dog walked away on its own. You really should see a doctor. Please, promise me you will."

I took a deep breath to calm down. "Sure, no problem."

"Don't just say it. Mean it. I'm worried you have a brain tumor or something."

"It's not a too-mah!" I said it in a German accent as a *Kindergarten Cop* reference, but I don't think Mom got it.

"Just promise me you'll do it."

"Okay, okay. I'll see a doctor." My next primary-care appointment was in nine months, so I'd bring it up then.

The rest of the evening was a bit strained. Everyone had lost their appetites, what with the hellhound attack and the brain-tumor talk. So, we cleaned up the monumental mess from the crab meal, and Cory, Sophie, and I quickly made excuses for why we had to head home without eating Mom's blueberry pie.

She made us take the pie home. And when we exited the house, we found Cerberus had left a colossal present at her front door.

CHAPTER 24

LAND OF THE ELVES

Summer and I had a tradition of visiting the wilderness, forests in particular. She helped me get in tune with the Goddess in me and discover my ability to commune with trees and nature.

Today, she drove me to a state park we'd never visited together before because it was farther from town than the others. One hundred years ago, it had been a private estate before the land was donated. It featured botanical gardens, access to the Intracoastal Waterway, and miles of hiking trails through a variety of ecosystems and tree species.

It also featured glorious live oaks, each more than a century old. These trees grew wider than they did tall, with giant horizontal limbs covered in Spanish moss, ferns, and air plants.

Summer stopped on the trail in front of a particularly large one.

"Why are we stopping?" I asked.

"Can you become the Goddess whenever you want?"

"What do you mean?"

"Exactly what I said."

"I haven't quite mastered it yet. Sometimes, I become her when I least expect it. It's kind of embarrassing. It looks like I've frozen from a seizure or something while I'm off doing goddess stuff. Even if I'm gone for a long time, my body is unresponsive only for seconds—a minute, tops. When a loved one is attacked, my mother instinct kicks in, and I become the Goddess right away."

"Elves can do something similar," Summer said, "but when we go to Ehrendil, we don't leave our human bodies behind. That would be an evolutionary disadvantage."

I laughed nervously, unsure of where she was going.

"Where is Ehrendil?"

"I thought everyone had heard of it. I guess the English translation would be 'Land of the Elves.' Ever wonder why you never see elves aside from me?"

"The same reason people don't see faeries, werewolves, and other supernatural creatures."

"No. I mean, why *you* don't see us—you, who are part of the supernatural world."

"I just figured there weren't any elves around here. Aren't you guys mostly in northern climes?"

"Nope. Wherever there are woods and forests, there are elves. And wherever there are elves, it is Ehrendil." She smiled mischievously. Today, she seemed more elven than ever. "Become the Goddess, and I'll take you there."

I gestured at the surrounding trees. "In this forest?"

"Yes. And in this tree." She pointed at the live oak we stood before.

I was beginning to understand somewhat. As the Goddess, I could transport myself into the sewer and then bring Sophie out of it. I asked Summer if this was what she meant.

"Sort of. Similar concept. Now, go ahead and do your thing."

"Like I said, I'm not sure I can do it on demand."

"You're a goddess. You can do it."

I glanced around to make sure no one was coming along the trail. Then, I closed my eyes. I felt self-conscious with Summer staring at me. Turning away, I cleared my mind and centered my thoughts on the Goddess as I always did. But this time, I willed myself to leave my body. That's not something most people want to do, to leave their selves behind.

Something shifted inside me, and I stepped forward. I still stood in front of the tree, but I was here in a timeless moment—the past, present, and future all at once.

Summer took my hand and led me toward the tree's trunk. After a brief feeling of disorientation, like when going through a gateway, we stepped through a doorway in the tree's bark.

And we entered a giant hall filled with voices and laughter.

It was like a banquet hall with walls of natural wood and no windows. The room was so tall, shadows blocked any view of the ceiling. Light was provided by glowing white orbs. Many were on the long tables, illuminating the elves sitting there. Others were attached to the walls, and still more floated in the air at different heights, drifting slowly in random directions.

Summer and I stood on the raised threshold of the hall. She looked the same, except, now, her ears were pointy. I looked down to find I was wearing a gown of a white silk-like material. I had a necklace woven of flowers, and I touched a crown of oak leaves in my hair.

"Welcome to Ehrendil," Summer said to me in Elvish. She turned to the crowd and raised her voice. "Your Majesty, King Aiwin, I present the Goddess Danu."

The magic that allowed us to enter this world inside a tree must also have given me the ability to understand Elvish. And no, Elvish is not how a drunk guy pronounces the name of Elvis Presley.

The crowd of elves—there were hundreds—stood up at the tables and applauded. At the far end of the room, at a smaller table, a tall man in a white tunic with a green cape and silver crown, stood and held out his arms toward me.

"Queen Gaylia and I welcome you. We are blessed by your visit."

Summer led me down the stairs and through the center aisle of the room, past the applauding elves. We stopped beside the dais that held the king's table.

He had blond hair, as did most of the elves in the room. He was slim and angular, with a narrow nose and pointy ears. Though his features were delicate, he radiated strength, both physical and mental. He was swoon-worthy—not as radiantly beautiful as Raphael, but pretty darn handsome for a non-angel.

The queen was petite and pretty. She smiled at me in a guarded fashion. Surprisingly, she had black hair, braided tightly to her head.

King Aiwin made a pushing-downward gesture to quiet the crowd. Footmen pulled two chairs out from the royal table for Summer and me. Once the king sat, everyone else did.

The table was set with simple wooden plates and bowls, empty for now, while goblets made from gourds were constantly filled by the footmen, with what I did not know. It appeared the feast had not yet been served.

"Your king and queen live right here in Florida?" I whispered to Summer.

"No. They can visit any part of Ehrendil they want almost instantly. You see, just as all the trees in a forest are connected to one another, all the forests are connected, too."

"Wow." I couldn't think of anything else to say. One mind-blowing experience after another lately seemed to have damaged my vocabulary.

Suddenly, all eyes at our table were upon me.

"I must admit, Goddess Danu, we elves have not worshipped you," the king said. "We're not like our dark brethren, the Fae, with their pantheon of deities. We only worship the earth itself. She is our earth mother. And she is gravely ill. We turn to you to ask for help."

I didn't know how I was supposed to help, but I kept my mouth shut. After all, I was an earth-mother goddess. By definition, the health of our planet was the main part of my job responsibilities.

"I feel the earth's pain," I said. Yeah, it was rather lame, but I wasn't sure how to navigate this situation.

"Can you make her well again?"

So far, I'd battled vampires and demons. I'd healed a forest destroyed by a wildfire. I thought I'd done quite a bit, thank you. Healing the entire planet seemed like a lot to ask.

"If I have the cooperation of the creatures who live on earth. The intelligent ones, I mean."

"Many of the intelligent ones aren't very smart," the king replied. "We elves, however, will give everything we can. My people are completely at your service."

"Thank you." I smiled, hoping he wouldn't ask me any more questions.

The king clapped his hands. "Now, we feast."

Servers moved among the tables in the hall, filling gourds with drink and laying out trenchers of food. I was worried the elves might be vegetarian, but there were grilled meats and fish, as well as mushrooms and root vegetables. Bowls upon bowls of nuts and berries were passed around, along with sliced apples, pears, and oranges.

I sipped from my gourd drinking vessel. The liquid was alcoholic and tasted like mead. After my second glass, the elves and their impossible request were growing on me.

After the feast, I expected entertainment. But instead, various courtiers and petitioners gathered at our table, trying to get some time with the king. Summer explained that the king and queen regularly visited the many elf communities to hear their concerns and deliver judgments and decrees.

"Let me show you around," Summer said to me.

"I thought you lived in an apartment in town."

"I do. It's because I'm half-human and serve in the Memory Guild. And I'm also a member of the Elven League."

We walked up a staircase that wound around the walls of this space that seemed to rise endlessly from the banquet hall below. We passed the beginnings of hallways that extended in various directions as we ascended. I assumed they were inside the limbs of the tree.

"These are living quarters, classrooms, workshops, etcetera," Summer explained.

"Is this tree truly hollow?"

"For our purposes, yes. But if a human cut it down, or a hurricane snapped off a limb, it would look normal. The idea is to exist without humans knowing about us. I'm going to take you outside, and you'll see how we avoid witnesses spotting 'wee people' in the trees."

She opened a door off the staircase that hadn't been visible to me. At first, I saw only leaves and pieces of the sky. We stepped out onto a wide limb.

I was about to confess my fear of falling when I noticed I wasn't me anymore. I gripped the bark with four claws, and I was covered with gray fur.

I was a squirrel.

I also had great peripheral vision like squirrels do, with eyes on the sides of my head seeing in both directions to avoid predators. To my left, I saw Summer, a squirrel just like me, perched on the limb, her enormous puffy tail twitching.

Follow me, her voice said in my head. *It's easy*.

She scampered out on the limb away from the trunk, then climbed a branch that grew from it. I followed, hesitating at first, but quickly gaining confidence.

When Summer jumped to a nearby branch, I did so, too. The branch swayed slightly beneath our weight, but I felt safe.

Look around, she said.

It was a whole other world up here. The limbs, branches, and leaves below us blocked much of the view of the ground. There were layers upon layers of this world, each one filled with tiny details of birds and their nests, insects that might never visit the ground, acorns, air plants. In this tree alone, you could explore for hours, and within jumping distance were other trees and their own worlds.

You can travel through much of this forest without ever touching the soil, Summer said. *Some elf children spend their first years in trees before they explore the ground.*

Summer used her squirrel paw to open an invisible door in the trunk, and I followed her inside. We were both in our human-goddess and elf forms again on the staircase.

"I'll take you back to the human world now," Summer said, leading me back down the long, winding staircase.

"Won't that be rude of me, as a guest, to leave right now?"

She smiled. "The king and queen are busy enough with their petitioners. Plus, no one would expect a deity to hang out with us."

"Well, the food was excellent. And the mead was killer! I hadn't realized I could eat and drink in my goddess incarnation."

"A goddess can do whatever she wants."

"Thank you for introducing me to your people. I've never seen elves," I said, "except for you and the leader of the Elven League when I went to Executive Committee meetings."

"Full-blooded elves do mingle with humans out of necessity. They just conceal their ears or other telltale signs. Elves have rights, like humans, and we need to assert them. That's why we have a guild, too."

I sadly realized that the elves' habitats were shrinking and disappearing, while the human population increased and development spread. Here they were, passionate about saving a planet where they had less and less of a place in it.

"Summer, I promise, as Danu, that I'll do everything I can to heal the earth. It's a big adjustment to become a goddess. I was raised a Christian and have trouble identifying with pagan deities. Some are just abstract representations of ideas or forces of nature. Then you have gods, like in Ancient Greece, who interacted with humans and caused trouble. But they didn't seem to do much that was useful.

"Danu is a goddess who was virtually forgotten," I continued. "Without relevance, she had no power. That's why she needed a human vessel like me to return to the world. And she needed to return now—I needed to return—for the very reason you brought me out here."

"Because the earth needs to be healed."

"Exactly."

"Right now, you are Danu, but I feel like I'm speaking to Darla."

"We are the same. This is the modern world, and you can't have gods tossing city buses around, acting like superheroes. Danu can heal a forest all on her own, but she needs Darla to interact with the world in other ways. It can be awkward at times."

Like when we exited the tree to find Darla standing there, frozen, gaping at the live oak. At least she was in that state for mere seconds.

I entered her and was Darla again.

Summer drove me back to the inn where I had to prepare for Teatime. Then, Wine Hour. Next, healing the planet.

I repaired the Veil, for Pete's sake, but everyone keeps dumping work on me.

When I walked inside the inn, I felt better though. This ancient place into which I'd dumped so much money and so much work has given me meaning. I've complained about its ghosts, vampire, gargoyle, and the monsters invading seemingly every couple of weeks.

But the Esperanza Inn always gave me and my family the feeling it was named after.

Hope.

WHAT'S NEXT

Note from the author: By the conclusion of *An Angel's Touch*, Darla has successfully completed her major tasks. Now that she's increasingly taking on the role of the Goddess, she's often "absent" from her day-to-day life in San Marcos.

But there's so much more to explore in this world, as well as characters who deserve to grow. Therefore, I'm excited to announce a new series, a spin-off from the Memory Guild saga. "Memory Guild's Daughter" will prominently feature Darla's daughter, Sophie, in her new job as the enforcer for the supernatural guilds of San Marcos. Darla will also be a major character as she works with the elves to heal the earth. In fact, I will use dual points of view to follow the two characters through their adventures, their mother-daughter relationship, and the conflict between their distinctly different roles of healer and hit woman.

Book 1, *To Kill an Elf*, is coming soon. I hope you join us on this new journey! Check wardparker.com for updates.

In the meantime, check out these amusing adventures featuring Darla's cousin, Missy, a forty-something witch and home-health nurse for retired supernaturals:

The Freaky Florida series, beginning with *Snowbirds of Prey*: https://books2read.com/snowbirdsofprey

Monsters of Jellyfish Beach, beginning with *The Golden Ghouls*: https://books2read.com/thegoldenghouls

ACKNOWLEDGMENTS

I wish to thank my loyal readers, who give me a reason to write more every day. I'm especially grateful to Sharee Steinberg and Shelley Holloway for all your editing and proofreading brilliance. To my A Team (you know who you are), thanks for reading and reviewing my ARCs, as well as providing good suggestions. And to my wife, Martha, thank you for your moral support, Beta reading, and awesome graphic design!

ABOUT THE AUTHOR

Ward is the author of the Memory Guild midlife paranormal mystery thrillers. Memory Guild's Daughter, debuting soon, will continue the adventures.

He also writes Monsters of Jellyfish Beach, set in the same world as his Freaky Florida series.

Ward lives in Florida with his wife, several cats, and a demon who wishes to remain anonymous.

Connect with him on Facebook (wardparkerauthor), BookBub, Goodreads, or Threads (wardparker2223). Check out his books at wardparker.com.

PARANORMAL BOOKS BY WARD PARKER

Freaky Florida Humorous Paranormal Novels

Snowbirds of Prey

Invasive Species

Fate Is a Witch

Gnome Coming

Going Batty

Dirty Old Manatee

Gazillions of Reptilians

Hangry as Hell (novella)

Books 1-3 Box Set

The Memory Guild Midlife Paranormal Mystery Thrillers

A Magic Touch (also available in audio)
The Psychic Touch (also available in audio)
A Wicked Touch (also available in audio)
A Haunting Touch
The Wizard's Touch
A Witchy Touch
A Faerie's Touch
The Goddess's Touch
The Vampire's Touch
An Angel's Touch
A Ghostly Touch (novella)
Books 1-3 Box Set (also available in audio)

Monsters of Jellyfish Beach Paranormal Mystery Adventures

The Golden Ghouls
Fiends With Benefits
Get Ogre Yourself
My Funny Frankenstein
Werewolf Art Thou?

Printed in Great Britain
by Amazon